W9-AUF-157

Louis Buckley

Return To

Louis Buckley
663 So. Academy St.
Galesburg Ill.

WHEN THEY STRAINED ON THE ROPE, THE IMAGE
SUDDENLY TILTED.—*Page* 191.

Tom Swift in the City of Gold.

TOM SWIFT IN THE CITY OF GOLD

OR

Marvelous Adventures Underground

BY

VICTOR APPLETON

AUTHOR OF "TOM SWIFT AND HIS MOTOR-CYCLE," "TOM SWIFT AND HIS
AIRSHIP," "TOM SWIFT AND HIS WIRELESS MESSAGE,"
"TOM SWIFT AND HIS ELECTRIC RIFLE," ETC.

ILLUSTRATED

NEW YORK
GROSSET & DUNLAP
PUBLISHERS

BOOKS BY VICTOR APPLETON

TOM SWIFT AND HIS MOTOR-CYCLE
  Or Fun and Adventures on the Road
TOM SWIFT AND HIS MOTOR-BOAT
  Or The Rivals of Lake Carlopa
TOM SWIFT AND HIS AIRSHIP
  Or the Stirring Cruise of the Red Cloud
TOM SWIFT AND HIS SUBMARINE BOAT
  Or Under the Ocean for Sunken Treasure
TOM SWIFT AND HIS ELECTRIC RUNABOUT
  Or the Speediest Car on the Road
TOM SWIFT AND HIS WIRELESS MESSAGE
  Or the Castaways of Earthquake Island
TOM SWIFT AMONG THE DIAMOND MAKERS
  Or the Secret of Phantom Mountain
TOM SWIFT IN THE CAVES OF ICE
  Or the Wreck of the Airship
TOM SWIFT AND HIS SKY RACER
  Or The Quickest Flight on Record
TOM SWIFT AND HIS ELECTRIC RIFLE
  Or Daring Adventures in Elephant Land
TOM SWIFT IN THE CITY OF GOLD
  Or Marvelous Adventures Underground
TOM SWIFT AND HIS AIR GLIDER
  Or Seeking Platinum Treasure
        (Other Volumes in Preparation)

*12mo.   Cloth   Illustrated   Price, per volume, 50 cents,
                postpaid*

GROSSET & DUNLAP
PUBLISHERS   NEW YORK

Tom Swift in the City of Gold

CONTENTS

iv CONTENTS

TOM SWIFT IN THE CITY OF GOLD

CHAPTER I

WONDERFUL NEWS

"LETTER for you, Tom Swift."

"Ah, thanks, Mr. Wilson. This is the first mail I've had this week. You've been neglecting me," and the young inventor took the missive which the Shopton postman handed to him over the gate, against which Tom was leaning one fine, warm Spring day.

"Well, I get around as often as I can, Tom. You're not home a great deal, you know. When you're not off in your sky racer seeing how much you can beat the birds, you're either hunting elephants in Africa, or diving down under the ocean, or out in a diamond mine, or some such out-of-the-way place as that. No wonder you don't get many letters. But that one looks as if it had come quite a distance."

I

"So it does," agreed Tom, looking closely **at** the stamp and postmark. "What do you **make** out of it, Mr. Wilson?" and then, just as many other persons do when getting a strange letter, instead of opening it to see from whom it has come, Tom tried to guess by looking at the hand-writing, and trying to decipher the faint post-mark. "What does that say?" and the young in-ventor pointed to the black stamp.

"Hum, looks like Jube—no, that first letter's a 'K' I guess," and Mr. Wilson turned it upside down, thinking that would help.

"I made it out a 'G'," said Tom.

"So it is. A 'G'—you're right. Gumbo—Twamba—that's what it is—Gumba Twamba. I can make it out now all right."

"Well, where, for the love of my old geog-raphy, is Gumba Twamba?" asked the lad with a laugh.

"You've got me, Tom. Must be in Sweden, or Holland, or some of those foreign countries. I don't often handle letters from there, so I can't say. Why don't you open your letter and find out who its from?"

"That's what I ought to have done at first." Quickly Tom ripped open the much worn and frayed envelope, through the cracks of which some parts of the letter already could be seen, showing that it had traveled many thousand miles before it got to the village of Shopton, in New York State.

"Well, I've got to be traveling on," remarked the postman, as Tom started to read the mysterious letter. "I'm late as it is. You can tell me the news when I pass again, Tom."

But the young inventor did not reply. He was too much engaged in reading the missive, for, no sooner had he perused the first few lines than his eyes began to open wide in wonder, and his manner plainly indicated his surprise. He read the letter once, and then over again, and when he had finished it a second time, he made a dash for the house.

"I say dad!" cried Tom. "This is great! Great news here! Where are you, dad? Say, Mrs. Baggert," he called as he saw the motherly housekeeper, "where's father? I've got great news for him? Where is he?"

"Out in the shop, I think. I believe Mr. Damon is with him."

"And blessing everything as usual, from his hat to his shoe laces, I'll wager," murmured Tom, as he made his way to the shop where his father, also an inventor like himself, spent much of his time. "Well, well, I'm glad Mr. Damon is here, for he'll be interested in this."

Tom fairly rushed into the building, much of the space of which was taken up by machinery, queer tools and odd devices, many of them having to do with the manufacture of aeroplanes, for Tom had as many of them as some people have of automobiles.

"I say, dad!" cried Tom, waving the letter above his head, "what do you think of this? Listen to——"

"Easy there now, Tom! Easy, my boy, or you'll oblige me to do all my work over again," and an aged man, beside whom a younger one was standing, held up a hand of caution, while with the other hand he was adjusting some delicate piece of machinery.

"What are you doing?" demanded the son.

"Bless my scarf pin!" exclaimed the other man —Mr. Wakefield Damon—"Bless my rubbers, Tom Swift! What *should* your father be doing but inventing something new, as he always is. I guess he's working on his new gyroscope, though it is only a guess, for he hasn't said ten words to me since I came out to talk to him. But that's like all inventors, they——"

"I beg your pardon, Mr. Damon," spoke Mr. Swift with a smile, "I'm sure——"

"Say, can't you listen to me for five minutes?" pleaded Tom. "I've got some great news—simply great, and your gyroscope can wait, dad. Listen to this letter," and he prepared to read it.

"Who's it from?" asked Mr. Damon.

"Mr. Jacob Illingway, the African missionary whom you and I rescued, together with his wife, from the red pigmies!" cried Tom. "Think of that! Of all persons to get a letter from, and *such* a letter! *Such* news in it. Why, it's simply great! You remember Mr. and Mrs. Illingway; don't you Mr. Damon? How we went to Africa after elephant's tusks, with Mr. Durban the hunter, and how we got the missionaries away from those little savages in my airship—don't you remember?"

"I should say I did!" exclaimed Mr. Damon. "Bless my watch chain—but they were regular imps—the red Pygmies I mean, not the missionaries. But what is Mr. Illingway writing to you about now, Tom? I know he sent you several letters since we came back from Africa. What's the latest news?"

"I'll tell you," replied the young inventor, sitting down on a packing box. "It would take too long to read the letter so I'll sum it up, and you can go over it later."

"To be brief, Mr. Illingway tells of a wonderful golden image that is worshiped by a tribe of Africans in a settlement not far from Gumba

Twamba, where he is stationed. It's an image of solid gold——"

"Solid gold!" interrupted Mr. Swift.

"Yes, dad, and about three feet high," went on Tom, referring to the letter to make sure. "It's heavy, too, no hollows in it, and these Africans regard it as a god. But that's not the strangest part of it. Mr. Illingway goes on to say that there is no gold in that part of Africa, and for a time he was at a loss how to account for the golden image. He made some inquiries and learned that it was once the property of a white traveler who made his home with the tribe that now worships the image of gold. This traveler, whose name Mr. Illingway could not find out, was much liked by the Africans. He taught them many things, doctored them when they were sick, and they finally adopted him into the tribe.

"It seems that he tried to make them better, and wanted them to become Christians, but they clung to their own beliefs until he died. Then, probably thinking to do his memory honor, they took the golden image, which was among his possessions, and set it up as a god."

"Bless my hymn book!" exclaimed Mr. Damon. "What did they do that for?"

"This white man thought a great deal of the

image," said Tom, again referring to the letter, "and the Africans very likely imagined that, as he was so good to them, some of his virtues had passed into the gold. Then, too, they may have thought it was part of his religion, and, as he had so often wanted them to adopt his beliefs, they reasoned out that they could now do so, by worshiping the golden god."

"Anyhow, that's what they did, and the image is there to-day, in that far-off African village. But I haven't got to the real news yet. The image of solid gold is only a part of it."

"Before this traveler died he told some of the more intelligent natives that the image had come from a far-off underground city—a regular city of gold—nearly everything in it that was capable of being made of metal, being constructed of the precious yellow gold. The golden image was only one of a lot more like it, some smaller and some larger——"

"Not larger, Tom, not larger, surely!" interrupted Mr. Swift. "Why, my boy, think of it! An image of solid gold, bigger even than this one Mr. Illingway writes of, which he says is three feet high. Why, if there are any larger they must be nearly life size, and think of a solid gold statue as large as a man—it would weigh—well, I'm afraid, to say how much, and

be worth—why, Tom, it's imposible. It would
be worth millions—all the wealth of a world must
be in the underground city. It's impossible
Tom, my boy!"

"Well, that may be," agreed Tom. "I'm not
saying it's true. Mr. Illingway is telling only
what he heard."

"Go on! Tell some more," begged Mr. Damon.
"Bless my shirt studs, this is getting exciting!"

"He says that the traveler told of this underground city of gold," went on Tom, "though he
had never been there himself. He had met a
native who had located it, and who had brought
out some of the gold, including several of the
images, and one he gave to the white man in
return for some favor. The white man took it
to Africa with him."

"But where is this underground city, Tom?"
asked Mr. Swift. "Doesn't Mr. Illingway give
you any idea of its location."

"He says it is somewhere in Mexico," explained the lad. "The Africans haven't a very
good idea of geography, but some of the tribes-
men whom the white traveler taught, could draw
rude maps, and Mr. Illingway had a native
sketch one for him, showing as nearly as possible
where the city of gold is located."

"Tom Swift, have you got that map?" suddenly cried Mr. Damon. "Bless my pocketbook, but——"

"I have it!" said Tom quietly, taking from the envelope a piece of paper covered with rough marks. "It isn't very good, but——"

"Bless my very existence!" cried the excitable man. "But you're not going to let such a chance as this slip past; are you Tom? Are you going to hunt for that buried city of gold?"

"I certainly am," answered the young inventor quietly.

"Tom! You're not going off on another wild expedition?" asked Mr. Swift anxiously.

"I'm afraid I'll have to," answered his son with a smile.

"Go? Of course he'll go!" burst out Mr. Damon. "And I'm going with him; can't I, Tom?"

"Surely. The reason Mr. Illingway sent me the letter was to tell me about the city of gold. He thought, after my travels in Africa, that to find a buried city in Mexico would be no trouble at all, I suppose. Anyhow he suggests that I make the attempt, and——"

"Oh, but, Tom, just when I am perfecting my gyroscope!" exclaimed Mr. Swift. "I need your help."

"I'll help you when I come back, dad.   I want to get some of this gold."

"But we are rich enough, Tom."

"It isn't so much the money, dad.   Listen. There is another part to the letter.   Mr. Illingway says that in that underground city, according to the rumor among the African natives, there is not only gold in plenty, and a number of small gold statues, but one immense big one— of solid gold, as large as three men, and there is some queer mystery about it, so that white traveler said.   A mystery he wanted to solve but could not.

"So, dad, I'm going to search for that underground city, not only for the mere gold, but to see if I can solve the mystery of the big gold statue.   And if I could bring it away," cried Tom in great excitement as he waved the missionary's letter above his head, "it would be one of the wonders of the world—dad, for, not only is it very valuable, but it is most beautifully carved."

"Well, I might as well give up my gyroscope work until you come back from the city of gold, Tom, I can see that," said Mr. Swift, with a faint smile.   "And if you go, I hope you come back.   I don't want that mysterious image to be the undoing of you."

"Oh, I'll come back all right!" cried Tom confidently. "Ho! for the city of gold and the images thereof! I'm going to get ready to start!"

"And so am I!" cried Mr. Damon. "Bless my shoe strings, Tom, but I'm with you! I certainly am!" and the little man excitedly shook hands with Tom Swift, while the aged inventor looked on and nodded his head doubtfully. But Tom was full of hope.

CHAPTER II

FOR a few moments after Tom Swift had announced his decision to start for the city of gold, and Mr. Damon had said he would accompany the young inventor, there was a silence in the workshop. Then Mr. Swift laid aside the delicate mechanism of the new model gyroscope on which he had been working, came over to his son, and said:

"Well, Tom, if you're going, that means you're going—I know enough to predict that. I rather wish you weren't, for I'm afraid no good will come of this."

"Now, dad, don't be talking that way!" cried Tom gaily. "Pack up and come along with us." Lovingly he placed his arm around the bent shoulders of his father.

"No, Tom, I'm too old. Home is the place for me."

"Bless my arithmetic tables!" exclaimed Mr. Damon, "you're not so much older than I am, and I'm going with Tom. Come on, Mr. Swift."

"No, I can't put up with dangers, hardship and excitement as I used to. I'd better stay home. Besides, I want to perfect my new gyroscope. I'll work on that while you and Tom are searching for the city of gold. But, Tom, if you're going you'd better have something more definite to look for than an unknown city, located on a map drawn by some African bushman."

"I intend to, dad. I guess when Mr. Illingway wrote his letter he didn't really think I'd take him up, and make the search. I'm going to write and ask him if he can't get me a better map, and also learn more about the location of the city. Mexico isn't such a very large place, but it would be if you had to hunt all over it for a buried city, and this map isn't a lot of help," and Tom who had shown it to his father and Mr. Damon looked at it closely.

"If we're going, we want all the information we can get," declared the odd man. "Bless my gizzard, Tom, but this may mean a lot to us!"

"I think it will," agreed the young inventor. "I'm going to write to Mr. Illingway at once, and ask for all the information he can get."

"And I'll help you with suggestions," spoke Mr. Damon. "Come on in the house, Tom.

Bless my ink bottle, but we're going to have some adventures again!"

"It seems to me that is about all Tom does— have adventures—that and invent flying machines," said Mr. Swift with a smile, as his son and their visitor left the shop. Then he once more bent over his gyroscope model, while Tom and Mr. Damon hurried in to write the letter to the African missionary.

And while this is being done I am going to ask your patience for a little while—my old readers, I mean—while I tell my new friends, who have never yet met Tom Swift, something about him.

Mr. Swift spoke truly when he said his son seemed to do nothing but seek adventures and invent flying machines. Of the latter the lad had a goodly number, some of which involved new and startling ideas. For Tom was a lad who "did things."

In the first volume of this series, entitled "Tom Swift and His Motor Cycle," I told you how he became acquainted with Mr. Damon. That eccentric individual was riding a motor cycle, when it started to climb a tree. Mr. Damon was thrown off in front of Tom's house, somewhat hurt, and the young inventor took him in. Tom and his father lived in the village of Shopton, New York, and Mr. Swift was an inventor of note. His son followed in his footsteps. Mrs. Swift had been dead some years, and they had a good housekeeper, Mrs. Baggert.

Another "member" of the family was Eradi-cate Sampson, a colored man of all work, who said he was named "Eradicate" because he "eradicated" the dirt. He used to do odd jobs of whitewashing before he was regularly employed by Mr. Swift as a sort of gardener and watchman.

In the first book I told how Tom bought the motor cycle from Mr. Damon, fixed it up, and had many adventures on it, not the least of which was saving some valuable patent models of his father's which some thieves had taken.

Then Tom Swift got a motor boat, as related in the second volume of the series, and he had many exciting trips in that craft. Following that he made his first airship with the help of a veteran balloonist and then, not satisfied with adventures in the air, he and his father perfected a wonderful submarine boat in which they went under the ocean for sunken treasure.

The automobile industry was fast forging to the front when Tom came back from his trip under water, and naturally he turned his attention to that. But he made an electric car instead of one that was operated by gasolene, and it proved to be the speediest car on the road.

The details of Tom Swift and his wireless message will be found in the book of that title. It tells how he saved the castaways of Earthquake Island, and among them was Mr. Nestor, the father of Mary, a girl whom Tom thought—but there, I'm not going to be mean, and tell on a good fellow. You can guess what I'm hinting at, I think.

It was when Tom went to get Mary Nestor a diamond ring that he fell in with Mr. Barcoe Jenks, who eventually took Tom off on a search for the diamond makers, and he and Tom, with some friends, discovered the secret of phantom mountain.

One would have thought that these adventures would have been enough for Tom Swift, but, like Alexander, he sighed for new worlds to conquer. How he went to the caves of ice in search of treasure, and how his airship was wrecked is told in the eighth volume of the series, and in the next is related the details of his swift sky-racer, in which he and Mr. Damon made a wonderfully fast trip, and brought a doctor to Mr. Swift in time to save the life of the aged inventor.

It was when Tom invented a wonderful electric rifle, and went to Africa with a Mr. Durban, a great hunter, to get elephants' tusks, that he rescued Mr. and Mrs. Illingway, the missionaries, who were held captive by red pygmies.

That was a startling trip, and full of surprises. Tom took with him to the dark continent a new airship, the *Black Hawk,* and but for this he and his friends never would have escaped from the savages and the wild beasts.

As it was, they had a hazardous time getting the missionary and his wife away from the jungle. It was this same missionary who, as told in the first chapter of this book, sent Tom the letter about the city of gold. Mr. Illingway and his wife wanted to stay in Africa in an endeavor to Christianize the natives, even after their terrible experience, so Tom landed them at a white settlement. It was from there that the letter came.

But the missionaries were not the only ones whom Tom saved from the red pygmies. Andy Foger, a Shopton youth, was Tom's enemy, and he had interfered with our hero's plans on many trips. He even had an airship made, and followed Tom to Africa. There Andy Foger and his companion, a German were captured by the savages. But though Tom saved his life, Andy did not seem to give over annoying the young inventor. Andy was born mean, and, as Eradicate Sampson used to say, "dat meanness neber will done git whitewashed outer him—dat's a fack!"

But if Andy Foger was mean to Tom, there was another Shopton lad who was just the reverse. This was Ned Newton, who was Tom's particular chum. Ned had gone with our hero on many trips, including the one to Africa after elephants. Mr. Damon also accompanied Tom many times, and occasionally Eradicate went along on the shorter voyages. But Eradicate was getting old, like Mr. Swift, who, of late years, had not traveled much with his son.

When I add that Tom still continued to invent things, that he was always looking for new adventures, that he still cared very much for Mary Nestor, and thought his father the best in the world, and liked Mr. Damon and Ned Newton above all his other acquaintances, except perhaps Mrs. Baggert, the housekeeper, I think perhaps I have said enough about him; and now I will get back to the story.

I might add, however, that Andy Foger, who had been away from Shopton for some time, had now returned to the village, and had lately been seen by Tom, riding around in a powerful auto. The sight of Andy did not make the young inventor feel any happier.

"Well, Tom, I think that will do," remarked

Mr. Damon when, after about an hour's work, they had jointly written a letter to the African missionary.

"We've asked him enough questions, anyhow," agreed the lad. "If he answers all of them we'll know more about the city of gold, and where it is, than we do now."

"Exactly," spoke the odd man. "Now to mail the letter, and wait for an answer. It will take several weeks, for they don't have good mail service to that part of Africa. I hope Mr. Illingway sends up a better map."

"So do I," assented Tom. "But even with the one we have I'd take a chance and look for the underground city."

"I'll mail the letter," went on Mr. Damon, who was as eager over the prospective adventure as was Tom. "I'm going back home to Waterfield I think. My wife says I stay here too much."

"Don't be in a hurry," urged Tom. "Can't you stay to supper? I'll take you home to-night in the sky racer. I want to talk more about the city of gold, and plan what we ought to take with us to Mexico."

"All right," agreed Mr. Damon. "I'll stay, but I suppose I shouldn't. But let's mail the letter."

It was after supper, when, the letter having

been posted, that Tom, his father and Mr. Damon were discussing the city of gold.

"Will you go, even if Mr. Illingway can't send a better map?" asked Mr. Damon.

"Sure," exclaimed Tom. "I want to get one of those golden images if I have to hunt all over the Aztec country for it."

"Who's talking of golden images?" demanded a new voice, and Tom looked up quickly, to see Ned Newton, his chum, entering the room. Ned had come in unannounced, as he frequently did.

"Hello, old stock!" cried Tom affectionately. "Say, there's great news. It's you and me for the city of gold now!"

"Get out! What are you talking about?"

Then Tom had to go into details, and explain to Ned all about the great quantity of gold that might be found in the underground city.

"You'll come along, won't you, Ned?" finished the young inventor. "We can't get along without you. Mr. Damon is going, and Eradicate too, I guess. We'll have a great time."

"Well, maybe I can fix it so I can go," agreed Ned, slowly. "I'd like it, above all things. Where did you say that golden city was?"

"Somewhere about the central part of Mexico, near the city of——"

"Hark!" suddenly exclaimed Ned, holding up a hand to caution Tom to silence.

"What is it?" asked the young inventor in a whisper.

"Some one is coming along the hall," replied Ned in a low voice.

They all listened intently. There was no doubt but that some one was approaching along the corridor leading to the library where the conference was being held.

"Oh, it's only Mrs. Baggert," remarked Tom a moment later, relief showing in his voice. "I know her step."

There was a tap on the door, and the housekeeper pushed it open, for it had been left ajar. She thrust her head in and remarked:

"I guess you've forgotten, Mr. Swift, that Andy Foger is waiting for you in the next room. He has a letter for you."

"Andy Foger!" gasped Tom. "Here."

"That's so, I forgot all about him!" exclaimed Mr. Swift jumping up. "It slipped my mind. I let him in a while ago, before we came in the library, and he's probably been sitting in the parlor ever since. I thought he wanted to see you, Tom, so I told him to wait. And I forgot all about him. You'd better see what he wants."

"Andy Foger there—in the next room," murmured Tom. "He's been there some time. I wonder how much he heard about the city of gold?"

CHAPTER III

THE parlor where Mr. Swift had asked **Andy** to wait, adjoined the library, and there was **a** connecting door, over which heavy curtains were draped. Tom quickly pulled them aside and stepped into the parlor. The connecting door had been open slightly, and in a flash the young inventor realized that it was perfectly possible for any one in the next rom to have heard most of the talk about the city of gold.

A glance across the room showed Andy seated on the far side, apparently engaged in reading a book.

"Did you want to see me?" asked Tom sharply. His father and the others in the library listened intently. Tom wondered what in the world Andy could want of him, since the two were never on good terms, and Andy cherished a resentment even after our hero had rescued him from the African jungle.

"No, I didn't come to see you," answered

22

Andy quickly, laying aside the book and rising to face Tom.

"Then what——"

"I came to see your father," interrupted the red-haired bully. "I have a letter for him from my father; but I guess Mr. Swift misunderstood me when he let me in."

"Did you tell him you wanted to see me?" asked Tom suspiciously, thinking Andy had made a mistatement in order to have a longer time to wait.

"No, I didn't, but I guess your father must have been thinking about something else, for he told me to come in here and sit down. I've been waiting ever since, and just now Mrs. Baggert passed and saw me. She——"

"Yes, she said you were here," spoke Tom significantly. "Well, then it's my father you want to see. I'll tell him."

Tom hurried back to the library.

"Dad," he said, "it's you that Andy wants to see. He has a letter from Mr. Foger for you."

"For me? What in the world can it be about? He never wrote to me before. I must have misunderstood Andy. But then it's no wonder, for my head is so full of my new gyroscope plans. There is a certain spring I can't seem to get right——"

"Perhaps you'd better see what Andy wants," suggested Mr. Damon gently. He looked at Tom. They were both thinking of the same thing.

"I will," replied Mr. Swift quickly, and he passed into the library.

"I wonder how much Andy heard?" asked Ned, in a low voice.

"Oh, I don't believe it could have been very much," answered Tom.

"No, I stopped you just in time," rejoined his chum, "or you might have blurted out the name of the city near where the buried gold is."

"Yes, we must guard our secret well, Tom," put in Mr. Damon.

"Well, Andy couldn't have known anything about the letter I got," declared Tom, "and if he only heard snatches of our talk it won't do him much good."

"The only trouble is he's been there long enough to have heard most of it," suggested Ned. They could talk freely now, for on going into the parlor Mr. Swift had tightly closed the door after him. They could just hear the murmur of his voice speaking to Andy.

"Well, even if he does guess about the city of gold, and its location, I don't believe he'll try to go there," remarked Tom, after a pause.

A moment later they heard Mr. Swift letting

Andy out of the front door, and then the inventor rejoined his son and the others. He held an open letter in his hand.

"This is strange—very strange," he murmured.

"What is it?" asked Tom quickly.

"Why, Mr. Foger has written to me asking to be allowed to sell some of our patents and machines on commission."

"Sell them on commission!" exclaimed his son. "Why does a millionaire like Mr. Foger want to be selling goods on commission? It's only a trick!"

"No, it's not a trick," said Mr. Swift slowly. "He is in earnest. Tom, Mr. Foger has lost his millions. His fortune has been swept away by unfortunate investments, he tells me, and he would be glad of any work I could give him. That's why Andy brought the letter to-night. I just sent him back with an answer."

"What did you say, dad?"

"I said I'd think it over."

"Mr. Foger's millions gone," mused Tom.

"And Andy in there listening to what we said about the city of gold," added Ned. "No wonder he was glad the door was open. He'd go there in a minute, Tom, if he could, and so would Mr. Foger, if he thought he could get rich. He wouldn't have to sell goods on commission if he could pick up a few of the golden images."

"That's right," agreed Tom, with an uneasy air. "I wish I knew just how much Andy had heard. But perhaps it wasn't much."

The time was to come, however, when Tom was to learn to his sorrow that Andy Foger had overheard a great deal.

"Bless my bankbook!" exclaimed Mr. Damon. "I never dreamed of such a thing! Andy had every reason in the world for not wanting us to know he was in there! No wonder he kept quiet. I'll wager all the while he was as close to the open door as he could get, hoping to overhear about the location of the place, so he could help his father get back his lost fortune. Bless my hatband; It's a good thing Mrs. Baggert told us he was there."

They all agreed with this, and then, as there was no further danger of being everheard, they resumed their talk about the city of gold. It was decided that they would have to wait the arrival of another letter from Mr. Illingway before starting for Mexico.

"Well, as long as that much is settled, I think I'd better be going home," suggested Mr. Damon. "I know my wife will be anxious about me."

"I'll get out the sky racer and you'll be in

Waterford in a jiffy," said Tom, and he kept his word, for the speedy aeroplane carried him and his guest rapidly through the night, bringing Tom safely back home.

It was several days after this, during which time Tom and Ned had had many talks about the proposed trip. They had figured on what sort of a craft to use in the journey. Tom had about decided on a small, but very powerful, dirigible balloon, that could be packed in a small compass and taken along.

"This city may be in some mountain valley, and a balloon will be the only way we can get to it," he told Ned.

"That's right," agreed his chum. "By the way, you haven't heard any more about Andy; have you?"

"Not a thing. Haven't even seen him. None of us have."

"There goes Rad, I wonder if he's seen him."

"No, or he'd have mentioned it to me. Hey, Rad," Tom called to the colored man, what are you going to do?"

"Whitewash de back fence, Massa Tom. It's in a mos' disrupted state ob disgrace. I'se jest natchally got t' whitewash it."

"All right, Rad, and when you get through come back here. I've got another job for you."

"A'right, Massa Tom, I shorely will," and Rad limped off with his pail of whitewash, and the long-handled brush.

It may have been fate that sent Andy Foger along the rear road a little later, and past the place where Eradicate was making the fence less "disrupted." It may have been fate or Andy may have just been sneaking along to see if he could overhear anything of Tom's plans—a trick of which he was frequently guilty. At any rate, Andy walked past where Eradicate was white-washing. The colored man saw the red-haired lad coming and murmured:

"Dere's dat no 'count white trash! I jest wish Massa Tom was heah now. He'd jest natchally wallop Andy," and Eradicate moved his long-handled brush up and down, as though he were coating the Foger lad with the white stuff.

As it happened, Eradicate was putting some of the liquid on a particularly rough spot in the fence, a spot low down, and this naturally made the handle of his brush stick out over the sidewalk, and at this moment Andy Foger got there.

"Here, you black rascal!" the lad angrily exclaimed. "What do you mean by blocking the sidewalk that way? It's against the law, and I could have you arrested for that."

"No, could yo' really now?" asked Eradicate drawlingly for he was not afraid of Andy.

"Yes, I could, and don't you give me any of your back-talk! Get that brush out of the way!" and Andy kicked the long handle.

The natural result followed. The other end of the brush, wet with whitewash, described a curve through the air, coming toward the mean bully. And as the blow of Andy's foot jarred the brush loose, the next moment it fell right on Andy's head, the white liquid trickling down on his clothes, for Eradicate was not a miser when it came to putting on whitewash.

For a moment Andy could not speak. Then he burst out with:

"Hi! You did that on purpose! I'll have you in jail for that! Look at my hat, it's ruined! Look at my clothes! They're ruined! Oh, I'll make you pay for this!"

"Deed, an' it shore was a accident," said Eradicate, trying not to laugh. "You done did it yo'se'f!"

"I did not! You did it on purpose! Tom Swift put you up to this! I'll—I'll——"

But Andy had to stop and splutter, for some of the lime ran down off his hat into his mouth, and he yelled:

"I'll—I'll—Ouch! Phew! Woof! Oof! Oh!"

Then, in his rage, he made a blind rush for Eradicate. Now the colored man had no fear of Andy, but he did not want the pail of whitewash to upset, and the said pail was right in the path of the advancing youth.

"Look out!" cried Eradicate.

"I'll make you look out!" spluttered Andy. "I'll thrash you for this!"

Eradicate caught up his pail. He did not want to have the trouble of mixing more of the liquid. Just as he lifted it Andy aimed a kick for him. But he mis-calculated, and his foot struck the bottom of the pail and sent it flying from the hands of the colored man. Sent it flying right toward Andy himself, for Eradicate jumped back out of the way.

And the next moment a veritable deluge of whitewash was sprayed and splashed and splattered over Andy, covering him with the snowy liquid from head to foot!

CHAPTER IV

A PERILOUS FLIGHT

THERE was silence for a moment—there had to be—for Eradicate was doubled over with mirth and could not even laugh aloud, and as for Andy the whitewash running down his face and over his mouth effectually prevented speech. But the silence did not last long.

Just as Eradicate caught his breath, and let out a hearty laugh, Andy succeded in wiping some of the liquid from his face so that it was safe to open his mouth. Then he fairly let out a roar of rage.

"I'll have you put in jail for that, Eradicate Sampson!" he cried. "You've nearly killed me! You'll suffer for this! My father will sue you for damages, too! Look at me! Look at me!"

"Dat's jest what I'se doin', honey! Jest what I'se doin'!" gasped Eradicate, hardly able to speak from laughter. "Yo' suah am a most contrary lookin' specimen! Yo' suah is! Ha! Ha!"

"Stop it!" commanded Andy. "Don't you dare

31

laugh at me, after throwing whitewash on me."

"I didn't throw no whitewash on you!" protested the colored man. "Yo' done poured it over yo'se'f , dat's what yo' done did. An' I jest cain't help laughin', honey. I jest natchally cain't! Yo' look so mortally distressed, dat's what yo' does!"

Andy's rage might have been dangerous, but the very excess of it rendered him incapable of doing anything. He was wild at Eradicate and would willingly have attacked him, but the whitewash was beginning to soak through his clothes, and he was so wet and miserable that soon all the fight oozed out of him.

Then, too, though Eradicate was old, he was strong and he still held the long handle of the whitewash brush, no unformidable weapon. So Andy contented himself with verbal abuse. He called Eradicate all the mean names he could think of, ending up with:

"You won't hear the last of this for a long time, either. I'll have you, and your old rack of bones, your mule Boomerang, run out of town, that's what I will."

"What's dat? Yo' all gwine t'hab Boomerang run out ob town?" demanded Eradicate, a sudden change coming over him. His mule was his most beloved possession. "Lemme tell yo' one thing, Massa Andy. I'se an old colored man, an'

I ain't much 'count mebby. But ef yo' dare lay one finger on mah mule Boomerang, only jest one finger, mind you', why I'll—I'll jest natchally drown yo'—all in whitewash, dat's what I'll do!"

Eradicate drew himself up proudly, and boldly faced Andy. The bully shrank back. He knew better than to arouse the colored man further.

"You'll suffer for this," predicted the bully. "I'm not going to forget it. Tom Swift put you up to this, and I'll take it out of him the next time I see him. He's to blame."

"Now looky heah, honey!" said Eradicate quickly. "Doan't yo' all git no sich notion laik dat in yo' head. Massa Tom didn't tell me to do nothin' an I ain't. He ain't eben 'round yeh. An' annudder thing. Yo'se t' blame fo' this yo' own se'f. Ef yo' hadn't gone fo' t' kick de bucket it nebber would 'a happened. It's yo' own fault, honey, an' doan't yo' forgit dat! No, yo' better go home an' git some dry clothes on."

It was good advice, for Andy was soaking wet. He glared angrily at Eradicate, and then swung off down the road, the whitewash dripping from his garments at every step.

"Land a massy! But he suah did use up all mah lime," complained Eradicate, as he picked up the overturned pail. "I's got t' make mo'. But I doan't mind," he added cheerfully, and then, as he saw the woe-begone figure of Andy shuffling along, he laughed heartily, fitted the brush on the handle and went to tell Tom and Ned what had happened, and make more whitewash.

"Hum! Served him right," commented the young inventor.

"I suppose he'll try to play some mean trick on you now," commented Ned. "He'll think you had some hand in what Rad did."

"Let him," answered Tom. "If he tries any of his games I'll be ready for him."

"Maybe we'll soon be able to start for the city of gold," suggested Ned.

"I'm afraid not in some time," was his chum's reply. "It's going to take quite a while to get ready, and then we've got to wait to hear from Mr. Illingway. I wonder if it's true that Mr. Foger has lost his fortune; or was that only a trick?"

"Oh, it's true enough," answered Ned. "I heard some of the bank officials talking about it the other day." Ned was employed in one of the Shopton banks, an institution in which Tom and his father owned considerable stock. "He hasn't hardly any money left, and he may leave town and go out west, I heard."

"He can't go any too soon to suit me," spoke Tom, "and I hope he takes Andy with him."

"Your father isn't going to have any business dealings with Mr. Foger then?"

"I guess not. Dad doesn't trust him. But say, Ned, what do you say to a little trip in my sky racer? I want to go over to Waterford and see Mr. Damon. We can talk about our trip, and he was going to get some big maps of Central Mexico to study. Will you come?"

"I will this afternoon. I've got to go to the bank now."

"All right, I'll wait for you. In the meanwhile I'l be tuning up the motor. It didn't run just right the other night."

The two chums separated, Ned to go downtown to the bank, while Tom hastened to the shed where he kept his spedy little air craft. Meanwhile Eradicate went on whitewashing the fence, pausing every now and then to chuckle at the memory of Andy Foger.

Tom found that some minor adjustments had to be made to the motor, and they took him a couple of hours to complete. It was nearly noon when he finished, and leaving the sky racer in the open space in front of the shed, he went in the house to wash up, for his face and hands were begrimed with dirt and oil.

"But the machine's in good shape," he said to the housekeeper when she objected to his appear-

ance, "and Ned and I will have a speedy spin
this afternoon."

"Oh, you reckless boys! Risking your lives in
those aeroplanes!" exclaimed Mrs. Baggert.

"Why, they're safer than street cars!" declared
Tom with a laugh. "Just think how often street
cars collide, and you never heard of an aeroplane
doing that."

"No, but think what happens when they fall."

"That's it!" cried Tom gaily, "when they fall
you don't have time to think. But is dinner
ready? I'm hungry."

"Never saw you when you weren't," commented the housekeeper laughing. "Yes, you can
sit right down. We won't wait for your father.
He said he'd be late as he wants to finish something about his gyroscope. I never did see such
people as inventors for spoiling their meals," she
added as she put the dinner on the table.

Mr. Swift came in before his son had finished.

"Was Andy Foger here to see me again?" he
asked.

"No, why do you ask?" inquired Tom quickly.

"I just saw him out by the aeroplane shed,
and——"

Tom jumped up without another word, and
hurried to where his sky racer rested on its bi-
cycle wheels.

He breathed more easily when he saw that Andy was not in sight, and a hurried inspection of the aeroplane did not disclose that it had been tampered with.

"Anything the matter?" asked Mr. Swift, as he followed his son.

"No, but when you mentioned that Andy was out here I thought he might have been up to some of his tricks. He had a little trouble with Eradicate this morning, and he threatened to get even with me for it." And Tom told of the whitewashing incident.

"I just happened to see him as I was coming to dinner," went on the aged inventor. "He hurried off when he noticed me, but I thought he might have been here to leave another letter."

"No," said Tom. "I must tell Eradicate to keep his weather eye open for him, though. No telling what Andy'll do. Well, I must finish eating, or Ned will be here before I'm through."

A little later Ned arrived, and helped Tom start the motor. With a roar and a bang the swift little machine rapidly got up speed, the propellers whizing around so fast that they looked like blurs of light. The sky racer was held back by a rope, as Tom wanted to note the "pull" of the propellers, the force they exerted against the air being registered on a spring balance.

"What does it say, Ned?" cried the young inventor as he adjusted the carburettor.

"A shade over nine hundred pounds."

"Guess that'll do. Hop in, and I'll cast off from the seat."

This Tom frequently did when there was no one available to hold the aeroplane for him while he mounted. He could pull a cord, loosen the retaining rope, and away the craft would go.

The two chums were soon seated side by side and then Tom, grasping the steering wheel, turned on full power and jerked the releasing rope.

Over the ground shot the sky racer, quickly attaining speed until, with a deft motion, the young inventor tilted the deflecting rudder and up into the air they shot.

"Oh, this is glorious!" cried Ned, for, though he had often taken trips with Tom, every time he went up he seemed to enjoy it more.

Higher and higher they rose rose and then with the sharp nose of the craft turned in the proper direction they sailed off well above the trees and houses toward Waterford.

"Guess I'll go up a bit higher," Tom yelled into his chums ear when they were near their destination. "Then I can make a spiral glide to earth. I haven't practiced that lately."

Up and up went the sky racer, until it was well

over the town of Waterford, where Mr. Damon lived.

"There's his place!" yelled Ned, pointing downward. He had to yell to be heard above the noise of the motor. Tom nodded in reply. He, too, had picked out Mr. Damon's large estate. There were many good landing places on it, one near the house for which Tom headed.

The aeroplane shot downward, like a bird darting from the sky. Tom grasped the rudder lever more firmly. He looked below him, and then, suddenly he uttered a cry of terror.

"What is it?" yelled Ned.

"The rudder! The deflecting rudder! It's jammed, and I can't throw her head up! We're going to smash into the ground, Ned! I can't control her! Something has gone wrong!"

CHAPTER V

NEWS FROM AFRICA

BLANKLY, and with fear in his eyes, Ned gazed at Tom. The young inventor was frantically working at the levers, trying to loosen the jammed rudder—the rudder that enabled the sky racer to be tilted upward.

"Can't you do it?" cried Ned.

Tom shook his head hopelessly, but he did not give up. Madly he worked on, and there was need of haste, for every moment the aeroplane was shooting nearer and nearer to the eartth.

Ned glanced down. They were headed for the centre of a large grass plot and the bank employee found himself grimly thinking that at least the turf would be softer to fall on than bare ground.

"I—I can't imagine what's happened!" cried Tom.

He was still yanking on the lever, but it would not move, and unless the head of the aeroplane was thrown up quickly, to catch the air, and check its downward flight, they would both be killed.

"Shut off the engine and vol-plane!" cried Ned.

"No use," answered Tom. "I can't vol-plane when I can't throw her head up to check her."

But he did shut off the banging, throbbing motor, and then in silence they continued to fall. Ned had half a notion to jump, but he knew that would mean instant death, and there was just a bare chance that if he stayed in the machine it would take off some of the shock.

They could see Mr. Damon now. The odd man had run out of his house at the sight of the approaching aeroplane. He knew it well, for he had ridden with Tom many times. He looked up and waved his hand to the boys, but he had no idea of their danger, and he could not have helped them had he been aware of it.

He must have soon guessed that something was wrong though, for a moment later, the lads could hear him shout in terror, and could see him motion to them. Later he said he saw that Tom was coming down at too great an inclination, and he feared that the machine could not be thrown up into the wind quickly enough!"

"Here goes something—the lever or the rudder!" cried Tom in desperation, as he gave it a mighty yank. Up to now he had not pulled with all his strength as he feared to break some connecting rod, wire or lever. But now he must take every chance. "If I can get that rudder up even a little we're safe!" he went on.

Once more he gave a terrific pull on the handle. There was a snapping sound and Tom gave a yell of delight.

"That's the stuff!" he cried. "She's moving! We're all right now!"

And the rudder had moved only just in time, for when the aeroplane was within a hundred feet of the earth the head was suddenly elevated and she glided along on a level "keel."

"Look out!" yelled Ned, for now a new danger presented. They were so near the earth that Tom had over-run his original stopping place, and now the sky racer was headed directly for Mr. Damon's house, and might crash into it.

"All right! I've got her in hand!" said the young inventor reassuringly.

Tom tilted the rudder at a sharp angle to have the air pressure act as a brake. At the same time he swerved the craft to one side so that there was no longer any danger of crashing into the house.

"Bless my——" began Mr. Damon, but in the excitement he really didn't know what to bless, so he stopped short.

A moment later, feeling that the momentum had been checked enough to make it safe to land, Tom directed the craft downward again and came gracefully to earth, a short distance away from his eccentric friend.

"Whew!" gasped the young inventor, as he leaped from his seat. "That was a scary time while it lasted."

"I should say so!" agreed Ned.

"Bless my straw hat!" cried Mr. Damon? "What happened? Did you lose control of her, Tom."

"No, the deflecting rudder got jammed, and I couldn't move it. I must look and see what's the matter."

"I thought it was all up with you," commented Mr. Damon, as he followed Tom and Ned to the front end of the craft, where the deflecting mechanism was located.

Tom glanced quickly over it. His quick eye caught something, and he utered an exclamation.

"Look!" the young inventor cried. "No wonder it jammed!" and from a copper sleeve, through which ran the wire that worked the rudder, he pulled a small iron bolt. "That got between the sleeve and the wire, and I couldn't move it," he explained. "But when I pulled hard I loosened it."

"How did it fall in there?" asked Ned.

"It didn't *fall* there," spoke Tom quietly. "It was *put* there."

"*Put* there! Bless my insurance policy! Who did such a dastardly trick?" cried Mr. Damon.

"I don't know," answered Tom still quietly, "but I suspect it was Andy Foger, and he was never any nearer to putting us out of business than a little while ago, Ned."

"Do you mean to say that he deliberately tried to injure you?" asked Mr. Damon.

"Well, he may not have intended to hurt us, but that's what would have happened if I hadn't been able to throw her up into the wind when I did," replied Tom. Then he told of Mr. Swift having seen the red-haired bully near the aeroplane. "Andy may have only intended to put my machine out of working order," went on the young inventor, "but it might have been worse than that," and he could not repress a shudder.

"Are you going to say anything to him?" asked Ned.

"I certainly am!" replied Tom quickly. "He doesn't realize that he might have crippled us both for life. I sure am going to say something to him when I get back."

But Tom did not get the chance, for when he and Ned returned to Shopton,—the sky racer behaving beautifully on the homeward trip,—it was learned that Mr. Foger had suddenly left town, taking Andy with him.

"Maybe he knew I'd be after him," said Tom grimly, and so that incident was closed for the time being, but it was a long time before Tom and Ned got over their fright.

They had a nice visit with Mr. Damon, and talked of the city of gold to their heart's content, looking at several large maps of Mexico that the eccentric man had procured, and locating, as well as they could from the meager map and description they had, where the underground treasures might be.

"I suppose you are getting ready to go, Mr. Damon?" remarked Ned.

"Hush!" cautioned the odd man, looking quickly around the room. "I haven't said anything to my wife about it yet. You know she doesn't like me to go off on these 'wild goose chases' as she calls them, with you, Tom Swift. But bless my railroad ticket! It's half the fun of my life."

"Then don't you think you can go?" asked the young inventor eagerly, for he had formed a strong liking for Mr. Damon, and would very much regret to go without him.

"Oh, bless my necktie! I think I'll be able to manage it," was the answer. "I'm not going to tell her anything about it until the last minute,

and then I'll promise to bring her back one of
the golden images. She won't object then."

"Good!" exclaimed Tom. "I hope we can all
bring back some of the images."

"Yes, I know who you'll bring one for," said
Ned with a laugh, and he took care to get beyond
the reach of Tom's fist. "Her first name is
Mary," he added.

"You get out!" laughed Tom, blushing at the
same time.

"Ah! What a thing it is to be young!" exclaimed Mr. Damon with a mock sigh. The boys
laughed, for the od man, though well along in
years, was a boy at heart.

They talked at some length, speculating when
they might hear from Mr. Illingway, and discussing the sort of an outfit that would be best
to take with them.

Then, as the afternoon was drawing to a close,
Tom and Ned went back in the aeroplane, hearing the news about the Fogers as I have previously
mentioned.

"Well, I'll have to wait until I do see Andy to
take it out of his hide," remarked Tom grimly.
"I'm glad he's out of the way, though. There
won't be any more danger of his overhearing our
plans, and I can work in peace on the dirigible
balloon."

Though Tom had many air crafts, the one he thought best suited to take with them on their search for the city of gold would have to be constructed from parts of several machines, and it would take some time.

Tom began work on it the next day, his father helping him, as did Mr. Damon and Ned occasionally. Several weeks were spent in this way, meanwhile the mails being anxiously watched for news from Africa.

"Here you are, Tom!" called the postman one morning, as he walked out to the shop where the young inventor was busy over the balloon. "Here's another letter from that Buggy-wuggy place."

"Oh, you mean Gumba Twamba, in Africa!" laughed the lad. "Good! That's what I've been waiting for. Now to see what the missionary says."

"I hope you're not going to go as a missionary to Africa, Tom," said the postman.

"No danger. This is just a letter from a friend there. He sent me some facts so I can go off on another expedition."

"Oh, you're always going off on wild adventures," commented Uncle Sam's messenger with a shake of his head as he hurried away, while Tom tore open the letter from Africa and eagerly read it.

CHAPTER VI

"BEWARE THE HEAD-HUNTERS!"

"THAT's what I want!" exclaimed the young inventor, as he finished the perusal of the missionary's missive.

"What is it?" asked Mr. Swift, entering the shop at that moment.

"News from Africa, dad. Mr. Illingway went to a lot of trouble to get more information for us about the city of gold, and he sends a better map. It seems there was one among the effects of the white man who died near where Mr. Illingway has his mission. With this map, and what additional information I have, we ought to locate the underground city. Look, dad," and the lad showed the map.

"Humph!" exclaimed Mr. Swift with a smile. "I don't call that a very clear map. It shows a part of Central Mexico, that's true, but it's on such a small scale I don't see how you're going to tell anything by it."

"But I have a description," explained Tom.

"It seems according to Mr. Illingway's letter, that you have to go to the coast and strike into the interior until you are near the old city of Poltec. That used to be it's name, but Mr. Illingway says it may be abandoned now, or the name changed. But I guess we can find it.

"Then, according to what he could learn from the African natives, who talked with the white man, the best way is to hire ox carts and strike into the jungle. That's the only way to carry our baggage, and the dirigible balloon which I'm going to take along."

"Pretty uncertain way to look for a buried city of gold," commented Mr. Swift. "But I suppose even if you don't find it you'll have the fun of searching for it, Tom."

"But we *are* going to find it!" the lad declared. We'll get there, you'll see!"

"But how are you going to know it when you see it?" asked his father. "If it's underground even a balloon won't help you much."

"It's true it is underground," agreed Tom, "but there must be an entrance to it somewhere, and I'm going to hunt for that entrance. Mr. Illingway writes that the city is a very old one, and was built underground by the priests of some people allied to the Aztecs. They wanted a refuge in times of war and they also hid their valuables there. They must have been rich to have so much gold, or else they didn't value it as we do."

"That might be so," assented Mr. Swift. "But I still maintain, Tom, that it's like looking for a needle in a haystack."

"Still, I'm going to have a try for it," asserted the lad. "If I can once locate the plain of the big temple I'll be near the entrance to the underground city."

"What is the 'plain of the big temple,' Tom?"

"Mr. Illingway writes," said the lad, again referring to the letter, "that somewhere near the beginning of the tunnel that leads into the city of gold, there is an immense flat plain, on which the ancient Aztecs once built a great temple. Maybe they worshiped the golden images there. Anyhow the temple is in ruins now, near an overgrown jungle, according to the stories the white man used to tell. He once got as near the city of gold as the big temple, but hostile natives drove him and his party back. Then he went to Africa after getting an image from someone, and died there. So no one since has ever found the city of gold."

"Well, I hope you do, Tom, but I doubt it. However, I suppose you will hurry your preparations for going away, now that you have all the information you can get."

"Right, dad. I must send word to Mr. Damon and Ned at once. A few more days' work, and my balloon will be in shape for a trial flight, and then I can take it apart, pack it up, and ship it. Then ho! for the city of gold!"

Mr. Swift smiled at his son's enthusiasm, but he did not check it. He knew Tom too well for that.

Naturally Mr. Damon and Ned were delighted with th additional information the missionary had sent, and Ned agreed with Tom that it was a mere matter of diligent search to find the underground city.

"Bless my collar button!" cried Mr. Damon. "It may not be as easy as all that, but Tom Swift isn't the kind that gives up! We'll get there!"

Meanwhile Tom worked diligently on his balloon. He sent a letter of thanks to Mr. Illingway, at the same time requesting that if any more information was obtained within the next three weeks to cable it, as there would not be time for a letter to reach Shopton ere Tom planned to leave for Mexico.

The following days were busy ones for all. There was much to be done, and Tom worked night and day. They had to get rifles ready, for they were going into a part of the country where they might meet hostile natives. Then, too, they had to arrange for the proper clothing, and other supplies.

To take apart and ship the balloon was no small task, and then there were the passages to engage on a steamer that would land them at the nearest point to strike into the interior, the question of transportation after reaching Mexico, and many other matters to consider.

But gradually things began to shape themselves and it looked as though the expedition could start for the city of gold in about two weeks after the receipt of the second letter from the missionary.

"I think I'll give the balloon a trial to-morrow," said Tom one night, after a hard day's work. "It's all ready, and it ought to work pretty good. It will be just what we need to sail over some dense jungle and land down on the plain by the great temple."

"Bless my slipers!" exclaimed Mr. Damon. "I must think up some way of telling my wife that I'm going."

"Haven't you told her yet?" asked Ned.

The ecentric man shook his head.

"I haven't had a good chance," he said, "but I think I'll tell her to-morrow, and promise her one of the gold images. Then she won't mind."

Tom was just a little bit nervous when he got ready for a trial flight in the new dirigible balloon. To tell the truth he much preferred aero-planes to balloons, but he realized that in a country where the jungle growth prevailed, and where there might be no level places to get a "take off," or a starting place for an aeroplane, the balloon was more feasible.

But he need have had no fears, for the balloon worked perfectly. In the bag Tom used a new gas, much more powerful even than hydrogen, and which he could make from chemicals that could easily be carried on their trip.

The air craft was small but powerful, and could easily carry Tom, Ned and Mr. Damon, together with a quantity of food and other supplies. They intended to use it by starting from the place where they would leave the most of their baggage, after getting as near to the city of gold as they could by foot trails. Tom hoped to establish a camp in the interior of Mexico, and make trips off in different directions to search for the ruined temple. If unsuccessful they could sail back each night, and, if he should discover the entrance to the buried city there was food enough in the car of the balloon to enable them to stay away from camp for a week or more.

In order to give the balloon a good test, Tom took up with him not only Ned and Mr. Damon, but Eradicate and Mr. Swift to equalize the weight of food and supplies that later would be carried. The test showed that the craft more than came up to expectations, though the trial trip was a little marred by the nervousness of the colored man.

"I doan't jest laik dis yeah kind of travelin'," said Eradicate. "I'd radder be on de ground."

Most of the remaining two weeks were spent in packing the balloon for shipment, and then the travelers got their own personal equipment ready. They put up some condensed food, but they depended on getting the major portion in Mexico.

It was two days before they were to start. Their passage had been engaged on a steamer, and the balloon and most of their effects had been shipped. Mr. Damon had broken the news to his wife, and she had consented to allow him to go, though she said it would be for the last time.

"But if I bring her back a nice, big, gold image I know she'll let me go on other trips with you, Tom," said the eccentric man. "Bless my yard stick, if I couldn't go off on an adventure now and then I don't know what I'd do."

They were in the library of the Swift home that evening, Tom, Ned, Mr. Damon and the aged inventor, and of course the only thing talked of was the prospective trip to the city of gold.

"What I can't understand," Mr. Swift was

saying, "is why the natives made so many of the same images of gold, and why there is that large one in the underground place. What did they want of it?"

"That's part of the mystery we hope to solve," said Tom. "I'm going to bring that big image home with me if I can. I guess——"

He was interrupted by a ring at the front door.

"I hope that isn't Andy Foger," remarked Ned.

"No danger," replied Tom. "He'll keep away from here after what he did to my aeroplane."

Mrs. Baggert went to the door.

"A message for you, Tom," she announced a little later, handing in an envelope.

"Hello, a cablegram!" exclaimed the young inventor. "It must be from Mr. Illingway, in Africa. It is," he added a moment later as he glanced at the signature.

"What does he say?" asked Mr. Swift.

"Can he give us any more definite information about the city of gold?" inquired Ned.

"I'll read it," said Tom, and there was a curious, strained note in his voice. "This is what it says:

" 'No more information obtainable. But if you go to the city of gold beware of the head-hunters!' "

"Head-hunters!" exclaimed Mr. Damon. "Bless my top-knot, what are they?"

"I don't know," answered Tom simply, "but whatever they are we've got to be on the lookout for them when we get to the gold city, and that's where I'm going, head-hunters or no head-hunters!"

CHAPTER VII

TOM MAKES A PROMISE

IT MAY well be imagined that the cable warning sent by Mr. Illingway caused our friends considerable anxiety. Coming as it did, almost at the last minute, so brief—giving no particulars—it was very ominous. Yet Tom was not afraid, nor did any of the others show signs of fear.

"Bless my shotgun!" exclaimed Mr. Damon, as he looked at the few words on the paper which Tom passed around. "I wish Mr. Illingway had said more about the head-hunters—or less."

"What do you mean?" asked Ned.

"Well, I wish he'd given us more particulars, told us where we might be on the lookout for the head-hunters, what sort of chaps they were, and what they do to a fellow when they catch him."

"Their name seems plainly to indicate what they do," spoke Mr. Swift grimly. "They cut off the heads of their enemies, like that interesting Filipino tribe. But perhaps they may not get after you. If they do——"

"If they do," interrupted Tom with a laugh,

"we'll hop in our dirigible balloon, and get above *their* heads, and then I guess we can give a good account of ourselves. But would you rather Mr. Illingway had said less about them, Mr. Damon?"

"Yes, I wish, as long as he couldn't tell us more, that he'd kept quiet about them altogether. It's no fun to be always on the lookout for danger. I'm afraid it will get on my nerves, to be continually looking behind a rock, or a tree, for a head-hunter. Bless my comb and brush!"

"Well, 'forewarned is forearmed,' " quoted Ned. "We won't think anything more about them. It was kind of Mr. Illingway to warn us, and perhaps the head hunters have all disappeared since that white traveler was after the city of gold. Some story which he told his friends, the natives in Africa, is probably responsible for the missionary's warning. Let's check over our lists of supplies, Tom, and see if we have everything down."

"Can't you do that alone, Ned?"

"Why?" and Ned glanced quickly at his chum. Mr. Damon and Mr. Swift had left the room.

"Well, I've got an engagement—a call to make, and——"

"Enough said, old man. Go ahead. I know what it is to be in love. I'll check the lists. Go see——"

"Now don't get fresh!" advised Tom with a laugh, as he went to his room to get ready to pay a little visit.

"I say, Tom," called Ned after him. "What about Eradicate? Are you going to take him along? He'd be a big help."

"I know he would, but he doesn't want to go. He balked worse than his mule Boomerang when I spoke about an underground city. He said he didn't want to be buried before his time. I didn't tell him we were going after gold, for sometimes Rad talks a bit too much, and I don't want our plans known.

"But I did tell him that Mexico was a great place for chickens, and that he might see a bull fight."

"Did he rise to that bait?"

"Not a bit of it. He said he had enough chickens of his own, and he never did like bulls anyhow. So I guess we'll have to get along without Rad."

"It looks like it. Well, go and enjoy yourself. I'll wait here until you come back, though I know you'll be pretty late, but I want to make sure of our lists."

"All right, Ned," and Tom busied himself with his personal appearance, for he was very particular when going to call on young ladies.

A little later he was admitted to her house by Miss Mary Nestor, and the two began an animated conversation, for this was in the nature of a farewell call by Tom.

"And you are really about to start off on your wild search?" asked the girl. My! It seems just like something out of a book!"

"Doesn't it?" agreed Tom. "However, I hope there's more truth in it than there is in some books. I should hate to be disappointed, after all our preparation, and not find the buried city after all."

"Do you really think there is so much gold there?"

"Of course there's a good deal of guesswork about it," admitted the young inventor, "and it may be exaggerated, for such things usually are when a traveler has to depend on the accounts of natives.

"But it is certain that there is a big golden image in the interior of Africa, and that it came from Mexico. Mr. Illingway isn't a person who could easily be deceived. Then, too, the old Aztecs and their allies were wonderful workers in gold and silver, for look at what Cortez and his soldiers took from them."

"My! This is quite like a lecture in history!" exclaimed Mary with a laugh. "But it's interesting. I wonder if there are any *small,* golden images there, as you say there are so many in the underground city."

"Lots of them!" exclaimed Tom, as confidently as though he had seen them. "I'll tell you what I'll do, Mary. I'll bring you back one of those golden images for an ornament. It would look nice on that shelf I think," and Tom pointed to a vacant space on the mantle. "I'll bring you a large one or a small one, or both, Mary."

"Oh, you reckless boy! Well, I suppose it *would* be nice to have two, for they must be very valuable. But I'm not going to tax you too much. If you bring me back two *small* ones, I'll put one down here and the other——"

She paused and blushed slightly.

"Yes, and the other," suggested Tom.

"I'll put the other up in my room to remember you by," she finished with a laugh, "so pick out one that is nicely carved. Some of those foreign ones, such as the Chinese have, are hideous."

"That's right," agreed Tom, "and I'll see that you get a nice one. Those Aztecs used to do some wonderful work in gold and silver carving. I've seen specimens in the museum."

Then the two young people fell to talking of the wonderful trip that lay before Tom, and Mary, several times, urged him to be careful of the dangers he would be likely to encounter.

Tom said nothing to her of the head hunters. He did not want to alarm Miss Nestor, and then, too, he thought the less he allowed his mind to dwell on that unpleasant feature of the journey, the less likely it would be to get on the nerves of all of them.

Ned was right when he predicted that Tom would make quite a lengthy visit. There was much to talk about and he did not expect to see Mary again for some time. But finally he realized that he must leave, and with a renewed promise to bring back with him the two small gold images, and after saying good-bye to Mr. and Mrs. Nestor, Tom took his leave.

"If you get marooned in the underground city, Tom," said Mr. Nestor, "I hope you can rig up a wireless outfit, and get help, as you did for us on Earthquake Island."

"I hope so," answered our hero with a laugh, and then, a little saddened by his farewell, and pondering rather solemnly on what lay before him—the dangers of travel as well as those of the head hunters—Tom hastened back to his own home.

The young inventor found Ned busy over the list of supplies, diligently checking it and com-

paring it with the one originally made out, to see
that nothing had been omitted. Mr. Damon had
gone to his room, for he was to remain at the
Swift house until he left with the gold-hunting
expedition.

"Oh, you've got back, have you?" asked Tom's
chum, with a teasing air. "I thought you'd given
up the trip to the city of gold."

"Oh, cheese it!" invited Tom. "Come on, now
I'll help you. Where's Eradicate? I want him to
go out and see that the shop is locked up."

"He was in here a while ago and he said he
was going to look after things outside. He told
me quite a piece of news."

"What was it?"

"It seems that the Foger house has been sold,
the furniture was all moved out to-day, and the
family has left, bag and baggage. I asked Rad
if he had heard where to, and he said someone
down in the village was saying that Andy and his
father have engaged passage on some ship that
sails day after to-morrow."

"Day after to-morrow!" cried Tom. "Why,
that's when ours sails! I hope Andy didn't hear
enough of our plans that night to try to follow
us."

"It would be just like him," returned Ned, "but
I don't think they'll do it. They haven't enough

information to go on. More likely Mr. Foger is going to try some new ventures to get back his lost fortune."

"Well, I hope he and Andy keep away from us. They make trouble everywhere they go. Now come on, get busy."

And, though Tom tried to drive from his mind the thoughts of the Fogers, yet it was with an uneasy sense of some portending disaster that he went on with the work of preparing for the trip into the unknown. He said nothing to Ned about it, but perhaps his chum guessed.

"That'll do," said Tom after an hour's labor. "We'll call it a night's work and quit. Can't you stay here—we've got several spare beds."

"No, I'm expected home."

"I'll walk a ways with you," said Tom, and when he had left his chum at his house our hero returned by a street that would take him past the Foger residence. It was shrouded in darkness.

"Everybody's cleared out," said Tom in a low voice as he glanced at the gloomy house. "Well, all I hope is that they don't camp on our trail."

CHAPTER VIII

ERADICATE WILL GO

"I GUESS everything is all ready," remarked Tom.

"I can't think of anything more to do," said Ned.

"Bless my grip-sack!" exclaimed Mr. Damon, "if there *is*, someone else has got to do it. I'm tired to death! I never thought getting ready to go off on a simple little trip was so much work. We ought to have made the whole journey from start to finish in an airship, Tom, as we've done before."

"It was hardly practical," answered the young inventor. "I'm afraid we'll be searching for this underground city for some time, and we'll only need an airship or a dirigible balloon for short trips here and there. We've got to go a good deal by information the natives can furnish us, and we can't get at them very well when sailing in the air."

"That's right," agreed the eccentric man. "Well, I'm glad we're ready to start."

It was the evening of the day before they were to leave for New York, there to take steamer to a small port on the Mexican coast, and every one was busy putting the finishing details to the packing of his personal baggage.

The balloon, taken apart for easy transportation, had been sent on ahead, as had most of their supplies, weapons and other needed articles. All they would carry with them were handbags, containing some clothing.

"Then you've fully made up your mind not to go; eh Rad?" asked Tom of the colored man, who was busy helping them pack. "You won't take a chance in the underground city?"

"No, Massa Tom, I's gwine t' stay home an' look after yo' daddy. 'Sides, Boomerang is gettin' old, an' when a mule gits along in yeahs him temper ain't none ob de best."

"Boomerang's temper never was very good, anyhow," said Tom. "Many's the time he's balked on you, Rad."

"I know it, Massa Tom, but dat jest shows what strong character he done hab. Nobody kin manage dat air mule but me, an' if I were to leave him, dere suah would be trouble. No, I cain't go to no underground city, nohow."

"But if you found some of the golden images you could buy another mule—two of 'em if you wanted that many," said Ned, and a moment later he remembered that Tom did not want the colored man to know anything about the trip after gold. He had been led to believe that it was merely a trip to locate an ancient city.

"Did yo' done say *golden* images?" asked Eradicate, his eyes big with wonder.

Ned glanced apologetically at Tom, and said, with a shrug of his shoulders:

"Well, I——"

"Oh, we might as well tell him," interrupted the young inventor. "Yes, Rad, we expect to bring back some images of solid gold from the underground city. If you go along you might get some for your share. Of course there's nothing certain about it, but——"

"How—how big am dem gold images, Massa Tom?" asked Eradicate eagerly.

"You've got him going now, Tom," whispered Ned.

"How big?" repeated Tom musingly. "Hum, well, there's one that is said to be bigger than three men, and there must be any number of smaller ones—say boy's size, and from that on down to the real little ones, according to Mr. Illingway."

"Real gold—yellow, gold images as big as a man," said Eradicate in a dreamy voice. "An'—an' some big as boys. By golly, Massa Tom, am yo' suah ob dat?"

"Pretty sure. Why, Rad?"

"Cause I's gwine wid yo', dat's why! I didn't know yo' all was goin' after gold. By golly I's gwine along! Look out ob mah way, ef yo' please, Mr. Damon. I'se gwine t' pack up an' go. Am it too late t' git me a ticket, Massa Tom?"

"No, I guess there's room on the ship. But say, Rad, I don't want you to talk about this gold image part of it. You can say we're going to look for an underground city, but no more, mind you!"

"Trust me, Massa Tom; trust me. I—I'll jest say *brass* images, dat's what I'll say—*brass!* We's gwine after *brass,* an' not *gold.* By golly, I'll fool 'em!"

"No, don't say anything about the images—brass or gold," cautioned Tom. "But, Rad, there's another thing. We may run across the head hunters down there in Mexico."

"Head hunters? What's dem?"

"They catch you, and chop off your head for an ornament."

"Ha! Ha! Den I ain't in no danger, Massa Tom. Nobody would want de head ob an old colored man fo' an ornament. By golly! I's safe from dem head-hunters! Yo' can't scare me dat way. I's gwine after some of dem gold images, I is, an' ef I gits some I'll build de finest stable Boomerang ever saw, an' he kin hab oats fo' times a day. Dat's what I's gwine t' do. Now look out ob mah way, Mr. Damon, ef yo' pleases. I's gwine t' pack up," and Eradicate shuffled off, chuckling to himself and muttering over and over again: "Gold images! Gold images! Images ob solid gold! Think ob dat! By golly!"

Think he'll give the secret away, Tom?" asked Ned.

"No. And I'm glad he's going. Four makes a nice party, and Rad will make himself useful around camp. I've been sorry ever since he said he wouldn't go, on account of the good cooking I'd miss, for Rad is sure a fine cook."

"Bless my knife and fork, that's so!" agreed Mr. Damon.

So complete were the preparations of our friends that nothing remained to do the next morning. Eradicate had his things all in readiness, and when good-byes had been said to Mr. Swift, and Mrs. Baggert, Tom, Ned and Mr. Damon, followed by the faithful colored man, set off for the depot to take the train for New York. There they were to take a coast steamer for Tampico, Mexico, and once there they could arrange for transportation into the interior.

The journey to New York was uneventful, but on arrival there they met with their first disappointment. The steamer on which they were to take passage had been delayed by a storm, and had only just arrived at her dock.

"It will take three days to get her cargo out, clean the boilers, load another cargo in her and get ready to sail," the agent informed them.

"Then what are we to do?" asked Ned.

"Guess we'll have to wait; that's all," answered Tom. "It doesn't much matter. We're in no great rush, and it will give us three days around New York. We'll see the sights."

"Bless my spectacles! It's an ill wind that blows nobody good," remarked Mr. Damon. "I've been wanting to visit New York for some time, and now's my chance."

"We'll go to a good hotel," said Tom, "and enjoy ourselves as long as we have to wait for the steamer."

CHAPTER IX

"THAT LOOKED LIKE ANDY!"

WHAT seemed at first as if it was going to be a tedious time of waiting, proved to be a delightful experience, for our friends found much to occupy their attention in New York.

Tom and Ned went to several theatrical performances, and wanted Mr. Damon to go with them, but the odd man said he wanted to visit several museums and other places of historical interest, so, while he was browsing around that way, the boys went to Bronx Park, and to Central Park, to look at the animals, and otherwise enjoy themselves.

Eradicate put in his time in his own way. Much of it was spent in restaurants where chicken and pork chops figured largely on the bills of fare, for Tom had plentifully supplied the colored man with money, and did not ask an accounting.

"What else do you do besides eat, Rad?" asked Ned with a laugh, the second day of their stay in New York.

"I jest natchally looks in de jewelery store windows," replied Eradicate with a grin on his honest black face. "I looks at all de gold ornaments, an' I tries t' figger out how much better man golden images am gwine t' be."

"But don't you go in, and ask what a gold image the size of a man would be worth!" cautioned Tom. "The jeweler might think you were crazy, and he might suspect something."

"No, Massa Tom, I won't do nuffin laik dat," promised Eradicate. "But, Massa Tom, how mucn *does* yo' 'spect a image laik dat *would* be worth?"

"Haven't the least idea, Rad. Enough, though, to make you rich for the rest of your life."

"Good land a' massy!" gasped Eradicate, and he spent several hours trying to do sums in arithmetic on scraps of paper.

"Hurrah!" cried Tom, when, on the morning of the third day of their enforced stay in New York, a letter was sent up to his room by the hotel clerk.

"What's up?" asked Ned. "I didn't know that you sent Mary word that you were here."

"I didn't, you old scout!" cried Tom. "This is from the steamship company, saying that the steamer *Maderia,* on which we have taken passage for Mexico, will sail to-night at high tide. That's

going to make the trip to Mexico it seemed, and later the boys learned that a tourist agency had engaged passage for a number of its patrons.

"That fat man will never get up the slope unless some one pushes him," remarked Ned, pointing to a very fleshy individual who was struggling up the steep gangplank, carrying a heavy valise. For the tide was almost at flood and the deck of the steamer was much elevated. Indeed it seemed at one moment as if the heavy-weight passenger would slide backward instead of getting aboard.

"Go give him a hand, Rad," suggested Tom, and the colored man obligingly relieved the fat man of his grip, thereby enabling him to give all his attention to getting up the plank.

And it was this simple act on the part of Rad that was the cause of an uneasy suspicion coming to Tom and Ned. For, as Eradicate hastened to help the stout passenger, two others behind him, a man and a boy, started preciptably at the sight of the colored helper. So confused were they that it was noticed by Ned and his chum.

"Look at that!" said Ned in a low voice, their attention drawn from the fat man to the man and youth immediately behind him. "You'd think they were afraid of meeting Rad."

"That's right," agreed Tom, for the man and

youth had halted, and seemed about to turn back. Then the man, with a quick gesture, tossed a steamer rug he was carrying over his shoulder up so that it hid his face. At the same time the lad with him, evidently in obedience to some command, pulled his cap well down over his face and turned up the collar of a light overcoat he was wearing. He also seemed to shrink down, almost as if he were deformed.

"Say!" began Ned in wondering tones, "Tom, doesn't that look like——"

"Andy Foger and his father!" burst out the young inventor in a horse whisper. "Ned, do you think it's possible?"

"Hardly, and yet——"

Ned paused in his answer to look more closely at the two who had aroused the suspicions of himself and Tom. But they had now crowded so close up behind the fat man whom Eradicate was assisting up the plank, that he partly hid them from sight, and the action of the two in covering their faces further aided them in disguising themselves, if such was their intention.

"Oh, it can't be!" declared Tom. "If they were going to follow us they wouldn't dare go on the same steamer. It must be some one else. But it sure did look like Andy at first."

"That's what I say," came from Ned. "But we can easily find out."

"How?"

"Ask the purser to show us the passenger list. Even if they are down under some other names he'd know the Fogers if we described them to him."

"That's right, we'll do it."

By this time the fat man, who was being assisted by Eradicate had reached the top of the gang plank. He must have been expected, for several friends rushed to greet him, and for a moment there was a confusing little throng at the place where the passengers came abroad. Tom and Ned hurried up, intent on getting a closer view of the man and youth who seemed so anxious to escape observation.

But several persons got in their way, and the two mysterious ones taking advantage of the confusion, slipped down a companionway to their stateroom, so that when our two lads managed to extricate themselves from the throng around the fat man, who insisted on thanking them for allowing Eradicate to help him, it was too late to effect any identification, at least for the time being.

"But we'll go to the purser," said Tom. "If

Andy and his father are on this steamer we want to know it."

"That's right," agreed Ned.

Just then there was the usual cry:

"All ashore that's going ashore! Last warning!"

A bell rang, there was a hoarse whistle, the rattle of the gangplank being drawn in, a quiver through the whole length of the ship, and Tom cried:

"We're off!"

"Yes," added Ned, "if Andy and his father are here it's too late to leave them behind now!"

CHAPTER X

MYSTERIOUS PASSENGERS

NED and Tom did not escape the usual commotion that always attends the sailing of a large steamer. The people on the dock were waving farewells to those on the boat, and those on the deck of the *Maderia* shook their handkerchiefs, their steamer rugs, their hands, umbrellas—in short anything to indicate their feelings. It was getting dark, but big electric lights made the dock and the steamer's deck brilliantly aglow.

The big whistle was blowing at intervals to warn other craft that the steamer was coming out of her slip. Fussy little tugs were pushing their blunt noses against the sides of the *Maderia* to help her and, in brief, there was not a little excitement.

"Bless my steamer chair!" exclaimed Mr. Damon. "We're really off at last! And now for the land of——"

"Hush!" exclaimed Tom, who stood near the

odd gentleman. "You're forgetting. Some one might hear you."

"That's so, Tom. Bless my soul! I'll keep quiet after this."

"Mah golly!" gasped Eradicate as he saw the open water between the ship and the dock, "I can't git back now if I wanter—but I doan't wanter. I hope yo' father takes good care ob Boomerang, Massa Tom."

"Oh, I guess he will. But come on, Ned, we'll go to the purser's office now."

"What for? Is something wrong?" asked Mr. Damon.

"No, we just want to see if—er—if some friends of ours are on board," replied the young inventor, with a quick glance at his chum.

"Very well," assented Mr. Damon. "I'll wait for you on deck here. It's quite interesting to watch the sights of the harbor."

As for these same sights they possessed no attractions for the two lads at present. They were too intent on learning whether or not their suspicions regarding the Fogers were correct.

"Ror if they *are* on board," said Tom, as they made their way to the purser's office, "it only means one thing—that they're following us to get at the secret of the city of gold," and Tom whispered this last, even though there seemed to be no one within hearing, for nearly all the passengers were up on deck.

"That's right," agreed Ned. "Of course there's a bare chance, if those two were the Fogers, that Mr. Foger is going off to try and make another fortune. But more than likely they're on our trail, Tom."

"If it's them—yes."

"Hum, Foger—no, I don't think I have any passengers of that name," said the purser slowly, when Tom had put the question. "Let's see, Farday, Fenton, Figaro. Flannigan, Ford, Foraham, Fredericks—those are all the names in the 'Fs'. No Fogers among them. Why, are you looking for some friends of yours, boys?"

"Not exactly friends," replied Tom slowly, "but we know them, and we thought we saw them come aboard, so we wanted to make sure."

"They might be under some other name," suggested Ned.

"Yes, that is sometimes done," admitted the purser with a quick glance at the two lads, "it's done when a criminal wants to throw the police off his track, or, occasionally, when a celebrated person wants to avoid the newspaper reporters. But I hardly think that——"

"Oh, I don't believe they'd do it," said Tom quickly. He saw at once that the suspicions of the

purser had been aroused, and the official might
set on foot inquiries that would be distasteful to
the two lads and Mr. Damon. Then, too, if the
Fogers were on board under some other name,
they would hear of the questions that had been
put regarding them, and if they were on a legiti-
mate errand they could make it unpleasant for
Tom.

"I don't believe they'd do anything like that,"
the young inventor repeated.

"Well, you can look over the passenger list
soon," said the purser. "I'm going to post it in
the main saloon. But perhaps if you described
the persons you are looking for I could help you
out. I have met nearly all the passengers already"

"Mr. Foger is a big man, with a florid com-
plexion and he has a heavy brown moustache,"
said Ned.

"And Andy has red hair, and he squints,"
added Tom.

"No such persons on board," declared the official positively. "It's true we have several persons who squint, but no one with red hair—I'm
sure of it."

"Then they're not here," declared Ned.

"No, we must have been mistaken," agreed
Tom, and there was relief in his tone. It was

bad enough to have to search for a hidden city of gold, and perhaps have to deal with the head-hunters, without having to fight off another enemy from their trail.

"Much obliged," said the young inventor to the purser, and then the two lads went back on deck.

A little later supper was served in the big dining saloon, and the boys and Mr. Damon were glad of it, for they were hungry. Eradicate ate with a party of colored persons whose acquaintance he had quickly made. It was a gay gathering in which Tom and Ned found themselves, for though they had traveled much, generally it had been in one of Tom's airships, or big autos, and this dining on a big ship was rather a novelty to them.

The food was good, the service prompt, and Tom found himself possessed of a very good appetite. He glanced across the table and noted that opposite him and Ned, and a little way down the board, were two vacant chairs.

"Can't be that anyone is seasick already," he remarked to his chum.

"I shouldn't think so, for we haven't any more motion than a ferryboat. But some persons are very soon made ill on the water."

"If they're beginning thus early, what will happen when we get out where it's real rough?" Tom wanted to know.

"They'll sure be in for it," agreed Ned, and a glance around the dining saloon showed that those two vacant chairs were the only ones.

Somehow Tom felt a vague sense of uneasiness —as if something was about to happen. In a way he connected it with the suspicion that the Fogers were aboard, and with his subsequent discovery that their names were not on the passenger list. Then, with another thought in mind, he looked about to see if he could pick out the man and youth who, on coming up the gang plank, had been taken by both Tom and Ned to be their enemies. No one looking like either was to be seen, and Tom's mind at once went back to the vacant seats at the table.

"By Jove, Ned!" he exclaimed. "I believe I have it!"

"Have what—a fit of seasickness?"

"No, but those empty seats—the persons we saw you know—they belong there and they're afraid to come out and be seen."

"Why should they be—if they're not the Fogers. I guess you've got another think coming."

"Well, I'm sure there's something mysterious about those two—the way they hid their faces as

they came on board—not appearing at supper—
I'm going to keep my eyes open."

"All right, go as far as you like and I'm with
you. Just now you may pass me the powdered
sugar. I want some on this pie."

Tom laughed at Ned's matter-of-fact indiffer-
ence, but when the young inventor turned in to
his berth that night he could not stop thinking of
the empty seats—the two mysterious passengers
—and the two Fogers. They got all jumbled in
his head and made his sleep restless.

Morning saw the *Maderia* well out to sea, and,
as there was quite a swell on, the vessel rolled
and pitched to an uncomfortable degree. This
did not bother Tom and Ned, who were used to
sudden changes of equilibrium from their voyages in the air. Nor did Mr. Damon suffer. In
fact he was feeling fine and went about on deck
like an old salt, blessing so many new things that
he had many of the passengers amused.

Poor Eradicate did suffer though. He was
very seasick, and kept to his berth most of the
time, while some of his new friends did what
they could for him.

Tom had in mind a plan whereby he might
solve the identity of the mysterious passengers.
He was going to do it by a process of elimina-
tion—that is he would carefully note all on board

until he had fixed on the two who had aroused his suspicions. And he had to do this because so many of the passengers looked very different, now that they had on their ship "togs," than when first coming on board.

But the rough weather of the first day prevented the lad from carrying out his plan, as many of the travelers kept to their staterooms, and there were a score of vacant places at the tables.

The next day, however, was fine, and with the sea like the proverbial mill pond, it seemed that everyone was out on deck. Yet when meal time came there were those same two vacant seats.

"What do you think of it, Ned?" asked Tom, with a puzzled air.

"I don't know what to think, Tom. It sure is queer that those two—whoever they are—don't ever come to meals. They can't be seasick on a day like this, and they certainly weren't the first night."

"That's right. I'm going to ask one of the stewards where their stateroom is, and why they don't come out."

"You may get into trouble."

"Oh, I guess not. If I do I can stand it. I want to solve this mystery."

Tom did put his question to one of the dining saloon stewards and it created no suspicions.

"Ah, yes, I guess you must mean Mr. Wilson and his son," spoke the steward when he had referred to a list that corresponded with the numbers of the vacant places at the table. "They have their meals served in their stateroom."

"Why?" asked Tom, "are they ill?"

"I really couldn't say, sir. They prefer it that way, and the captain consented to it from the first."

"But I should think they'd want to get out for a breath of air," put in Ned. "I can't stay below decks very long."

"They may come out at night," suggested the steward. "Some of our travelers think they are less likely to be seasick if they come out at night. They don't see the motion of the waves then."

"Guess that's it," agreed Tom with a wink at Ned. "Much obliged. Glad we're not seasick," and he linked his arm in that of his chum's and marched him off.

"Why the wink?" asked Ned, when they were out of earshot of the steward.

"That was to tip you off to say nothing more. I've got a plan I'm going to work."

"What is it?"

"Well, we know who the mysterious ones are, anyhow—at least we know their names—Wilson."

"It may not be the right one."

"That doesn't make any difference. I can find out their stateroom by looking at the passenger list."

"What good will that do."

"Lots. I'm going to keep a watch on that stateroom until I get a good look at the people in it. And if they only come out at night, which it begins to look like, I'm going to do some night watching. This thing has got to be settled, Ned. Our trip to the city of gold is too important to risk having a mysterious couple on our trail— when that same couple may be the Fogers. I'm going to do some detective work, Ned!"

CHAPTER XI

THE MIDNIGHT ALARM

"WHEW! What a lot of 'em!"

"Bless my fish line! It's a big school!"

"Look how they turn over and over, and leap from the water."

"By golly, dere is suttinly some fish dere!"

These were the exclamations made by our four friends a few days later, as they leaned over the rail of the *Maderia* and watched a big school of porpoises gamboling about in the warm waters of the gulf stream. It was the second porpoise school the ship had come up with on the voyage, and this was a much larger one than the first, so that the passengers crowded up to see the somewhat novel sight.

"If they were only good eating now, we might try for a few," observed Ned.

"Some folks eat them, but they're too oily for me," observed a gentleman who had struck up an acquaintance with the boys and Mr. Damon. "Their skin makes excellent shoe laces though, and their oil is used for delicate machinery—especially some that comes from around the head, at least so I have heard."

"Wow! Did you see that?" cried Tom, as one large porpoise leaped clear of the water, turned over several times and fell back with a loud splash. "That was the biggest leap yet."

"And there goes another," added Ned.

"Say, this ought to bring those two mysterious passengers out of their room," observed Tom to his chum in a low voice. "Nearly everyone else seems to be on deck."

"You haven't been able to catch a glimpse of them; eh Tom?"

"Not a peak. I stayed up several nights, as you know, and paced the deck, but they didn't stir out. Or. if they did, it must have been toward morning, after I turned in. I can't understand it. They must be either criminals, afraid of being seen, or they *are* the Fogers, and they know we're on to their game."

"It looks as if it might be one or the other, Tom. But if they are criminals we don't have to worry about 'em. They don't concern us."

"No, that's right. Split mackerel! Look at that fellow jump. He's got 'em all beat!" and Tom excitedly, pointed at the porpoises, the whole school of which was swimming but a short distance from the steamer.

"Yes, a lot of them are jumping now. I wonder——"

"Look! Look!" cried the man who had been talking to Mr. Damon. "Something out of the ordinary is going on among those porpoises. I never saw them leap out of the water like that before."

"Sharks! It's sharks!" cried a sailor who came running along the deck. "A school of sharks are after the porpoises!"

"I believe he's right," added Mr. Sander, the gentleman with Mr. Damon. "See, there's the ugly snout of one now. He made a bite for that big porpoise but missed."

"Bless my meat axe!" cried the odd man. "So he did. Say, boys, this is worth seeing. There'll be a big fight in a minute."

"Not much of a fight," remarked Mr. Sander. "The porpoise isn't built for fighting. They're trying to get away from the sharks by leaping up."

"Why don't they dive, and so get away?" asked Ned.

"The sharks are too good at diving," went on Mr. Sander. "The porpoises couldn't escape that way. Their only hope is that something will scare the sharks away, otherwise they'll kill until their appetites are satisfied, and that isn't going to be very soon I'm afraid."

"Look! Look!" cried Ned. "A shark leaped half way out of the water then."

"Yes, I saw it," called Tom.

There was now considerable excitebent on deck. Nearly all the passengers, many of the crew and several of the officers were watching the strange sight. The porpoises were frantically tumbling, turning and leaping to get away from their voracious enemies.

"Oh, if I only had my electric rifle!" cried Tom. "I'd make some of those ugly sharks feel sick!"

"Bless my cartridge belt!" cried Mr. Damon. "That would be a good idea. The porpoises are such harmless creatures. It's a shame to see them attacked so."

For the activity of the sharks had now redoubled, and they were darting here and there amid the school of porpoises biting with their cruel jaws. The other fish were frantically leaping and tumbling, but the strange part of it was that the schools of sharks and porpoises kept about the same distance ahead of the ship, so that the passengers had an excellent view of the novel and thrilling sight.

"Rifle!" said Mr. Sander," catching at the

word. "I fancy the captain may have some. He's quite a friend of mine, I'll speak to him."

"Get me one, too, if you please," called Ned as the gentleman hurried away.

"And I'll also try my luck at potting a shark. Bless my gunpowder if I won't!" said Mr. Damon.

The captain did have several rifles in his stateroom, and he loaned them to Mr. Sander. They were magazine weapons, firing sixteen shots each, but they were not of as high power as those Tom had packed away.

"Now we'll make those sharks sing a different tune, if sharks sing!" cried the young inventor.

"Yes, we're coming to the rescue of the porpoises!" added Ned.

The passengers crowded up to witness the marksmanship, and soon the lads and Mr. Damon were at it.

It was no easy matter to hit a shark, as the big, ugly fish were only seen for a moment in their mad rushes after the porpoises, but both Tom and Ned were good shots and they made the bullets tell.

"There, I hit one big fellow!" cried Mr. Damon. "Bless my bull's eye, but I plugged him right in the mouth, I think."

"I hope you knocked out some of his teeth," cried Ned.

They fired rapidly, and while they probably hit some of the innocent porpoises in their haste, yet they accomplished what they had set out to do—scare off the sharks. In a little while the "tigers of the sea" as some one has aptly called them, disappeared.

"That's the stuff!" cried Mr. Damon. "Now we can watch the porpoises at play."

But they did not have that sight to interest them very long. For, as suddenly as the gamboling fish had appeared, they sank from sight—all but a few dead ones that the sharks had left floating on the calm surface of the ocean. Probably the timid fish had taken some alarm from the depths into which they sank.

"Well, that was some excitement while it lasted," remarked Tom, as he and Ned took the rifles back to the captain.

"But it didn't bring out the mysterious passengers," added Ned. Tom shook his head and on their return to deck he purposely went out of his way to go past Stateroom No. 27, where the "Wilsons" were quartered. The door was closed and a momentary pause to listen brought our hero no clew, for all was silent in the room.

"It's too much for me," he murmured, shaking his head and he rejoined his chum.

Several more days passed, for the *Maderia* was

a slow boat, and could not make good time to Mexico. However, our travelers were in no haste, and they fully enjoyed the voyage.

Try as Tom did to get a glimpse of the mysterious passengers he was unsuccessful. He spent many hours in a night, and early morning vigil, only to have to do his sleeping next day, and it resulted in nothing.

"I guess they want to get on Mexican soil before any one sees their faces," spoke Ned, and Tom was inclined to agree with his chum.

They awoke one morning to find the sea tempestuous. The ship tossed and rolled amid the billows, and the captain said they had run into the tail end of a gulf hurricane.

"Two days more and we'll be in port," he added, "and I'm sorry the voyage had to be marred even by this blow."

For it did blow, and, though it was not a dangerous storm, yet many passengers kept below.

"I'm afraid this settles it," remarked Tom that night, when the ship was still pitching and tossing. "They won't come out now, and this is likely to keep up until we get to port. Well, I can't help it."

But fate was on the verge of aiding Tom in an unexpected way. Nearly every one turned in early that night for it was no pleasure to sit in the saloons, and to lie in one's berth made it easier to stand the rolling of the vessel.

Tom and Ned, together with Mr. Damon, had fallen into slumber in spite of the storm, when, just as eight bells announced midnight there was a sudden jar throughout the whole ship.

The *Maderia* quivered from stem to stern, seemed to hesitate a moment as though she had been brought to a sudden stop, and then plowed on, only to bring up against some obstruction again, with that same sickening jar throughout her length.

"Bless my soul! What's that?" cried Mr. Damon, springing from his berth.

"Something has happened!" added Tom, as he reached out and switched on the electric lights.

"We hit something!" declared Ned.

The ship was now almost stopped and she was rolling from side to side.

Up on deck could be heard confused shouts and the running to and fro of many feet. The jangling of bells sounded—hoarse orders were shouted—and there arose a subdued hubbub in the interior of the ship.

"Something sure is wrong!" cried Tom. "We'd better get our clothes on and get on deck! Come on, Ned and Mr. Damon! Grab life preservers!"

CHAPTER XII

INTO THE UNKNOWN

"BLESS my overshoes! I hope we're not sinking!" cried Mr. Damon, as he struggled into some of his clothes, an example followed by Ned and Tom.

"This boat has water-tight compartments, and if it does sink it won't do it in a hurry," commented Tom.

"I don't care to have it do it at all," declared Ned, who found that he had started to get into his trousers hindside before and he had to change them. "Think of all our baggage and supplies and the balloon on board." For the travelers had shipped their things by the same steamer as that on which they sailed.

"Well, let's get out and learn the worst," cried Tom.

He was the first to leave the stateroom, and as he rushed along the passages which were now brilliant with light he saw other half-clad passengers bent on the same errand as himself, to get on deck and learn what had happened.

"Wait, Tom!" called Ned.

"Come along, I'm just ahead of you," yelled his chum from around a corner. "I'm going to see if Eradicate is up. He's an awful heavy sleeper."

"Bless my feather bed! That shock was enough to awaken anyone!" commented Mr. Damon, as he followed Ned, who was running to catch up to Tom.

Suddenly a thought came to our hero. The mysterious passengers in Stateroom No. 27! Surely this midnight alarm would bring them out, and he might have a chance to see who they were.

Tom thought quickly. He could take a turn, go through a short passage, and run past the room of the mysterious passengers getting on deck as quickly as if he went the usual way.

"I'll go look after Rad!" Tom shouted to Ned. "You go up on deck, and I'll join you."

Eradicate's stateroom was on his way, after he had passed No. 27. Tom at once put his plan into execution. As he ran on, the confusion on deck seemed to increase, but the lad noted that the vessel did not pitch and roll so much, and she seemed to be on an even keel, and in no immediate danger of going down.

As Tom neared Stateroom No. 27 he heard

voices coming from it, voices that sent a thrill through him, for he was sure he had heard them before.

"Where are the life preservers? Oh, I *know* we'll be drowned! I wish I'd never come on this trip! Look out, those are my pants you're putting on! Oh, where is my collar? Hand me my coat! Look out, you're stepping on my fingers!"

These were the confused and alarmed cries that Tom heard. He paused for a moment opposite the door, and then it was suddenly flung open. The lights were glaring brightly inside and a strange sight met the gaze of the young inventor.

There stood Mr. Foger and beside him—half dressed—was his son—Andy! Tom gasped. So did Andy and Mr. Foger, for they had both recognized our hero.

But how Mr. Foger had changed! His moustache was shaved off, though in spite of this Tom knew him. And Andy! No longer was his hair red, for it had been dyed a deep black and glasses over his eyes concealed their squint. No wonder the purser had not recognized them by the descriptions Tom and Ned had given.

"Andy Foger!" gasped Tom.

"Tom—it's Tom Swift, father!" stammered the bully.

"Close the door!" sharply ordered Mr. Foger, though he and his son had been about to rush out.

"I won't do it!" cried Andy. "The ship is sinking and I'm not going to be drowned down here."

"So it was you—after all," went on Tom. "What are you doing here?"

"None of your business!" snapped Andy. "Get out of my way, I'm going on deck."

Tom realized that it was not the proper time to hold a conversation, with a possibly sinking ship under him. He looked at Mr. Foger, and many thoughts shot through his mind. Why were they on board? Had it anything to do with the city of gold? Had Andy overheard the talk? Or was Mr. Foger merely looking for a new venture whereby to retrieve his lost fortune.

Tom could not answer. The bully's father glared at our hero and then, slipping on a coat, he made a dash for the door.

"Get out of my way!" he shouted, and Tom stood aside.

Andy was already racing for the deck, and as the noise and confusion seemed to increase rather than diminish, Tom concluded that his wisest move would be to get out and see what all the excitement was about.

He stopped on his way to arouse Eradicate but found that he and all the colored persons had left their staterooms. A few seconds later Tom was on deck.

"It's all right, now! It's all right!" several officers were calling. There is no danger. Go back to your staterooms. The danger is all over."

"Is the ship sinking?"

"What happened?"

"Are we on fire?"

"Are you sure there's no danger?"

These were only a few of the questions that were flying about, and the officers answered them as best they could.

"We hit a derelict, or some bit of wreckage," explained the first mate, when he could command silence. "There is a slight hole below the water-line, but the bulkheads have been closed, and there is not the slightest danger."

"Are we going to turn back for New York?" asked one woman.

"No, certainly not. We're going right on as soon as a slight break to one of the engines can be repaired. We are in no danger. Only a little water came in before the automatic bulkheads were shut. We haven't even a list to one side. Now please clear the decks and go back to bed."

It took more urging, but finally the passengers

began to disperse. Tom found Ned and Mr. Damon, who were looking for him.

Bless my life preserver!" cried the odd man. "I thought surely this was my last voyage, Tom!"

"So did I," added Ned. "What's the matter, Tom, you look as though you'd seen a ghost."

"I have—pretty near. The Fogers are on board."

"No! You don't mean it!"

"It's a fact. I just saw them. They are the mysterious pasengers." And Tom related his experience.

"Where are they now?" demanded Ned, looking about the deck.

"Gone below again, I suppose. Though I don't see what object they can have in concealing their identity any longer."

"Me either. Well, that surely is a queer go."

"Bless my hot cross buns! I should say so!" commented Mr. Damon when he heard about it. "What are you going to do, Tom?"

"Nothing. I can't. They have a right on board. But if they try to follow us—well, I'll act then," and Tom shut his jaws grimly.

Our three friends went back to their stateroom, and Eradicate also retired. The excitement was passing, and soon the ship was under way again, the sudden shock having caused slight damage to one of the big engines. But it was soon repaired and, though the storm still continued, the ship made her way well through the waves.

A stout bow, water-tight compartments, and the fact (learned later) that she had struck the derelict a glancing blow, had combined to save the *Maderia*.

There were many curious ones who looked over the side next morning to see the gaping hole in the bow. A canvas had been rigged over it, however, to keep out the waves as much as possible, so little could be viewed. Then the thoughts of landing occupied the minds of all, and the accident was nearly forgotten. For it was announced that they would dock early the next morning.

In spite of the fact that their presence on board was known to Tom and his friends, the Fogers still kept to their stateroom, not even appearing at meals. Tom wondered what their object could be, but could not guess.

"Well, here we are at last—in Mexico," exclaimed Ned the next morning, when, the *Maderia* having docked, allowed the passengers to disembark, a clean bill of health having been her good luck.

"Yes, and now for a lot of work!" added Tom.

"We've got to see about getting ox teams, carts and helpers, and no end of food for our trip into the interior."

"Bless my coffee pot! It's like old times to be going off into the jungle or wilderness camping," said Mr. Damon.

"Did you see anything of the Fogers?" asked Ned of his chum.

"Not a thing. Guess they're in their stateroom, and they can stay there for all of me. I'm going to get busy."

Tom and his friends went to a hotel, for they knew it would take several days to get their expedition in shape. They looked about for a sight of their enemies, but saw nothing of them.

It took five days to hire the ox carts, get helpers, a supply of food and other things, and to unload the balloon and baggage from the ship. In all this time there was no sign of the Fogers, and Tom hoped they had gone about their own business.

Our friends had let it be known that they were going into the interior to prospect, look for historic relics and ruins, and generally have a sort of vacation.

"For if it is even hinted that we are after the city of gold," said Tom, "it would be all up with us. The whole population of Mexico would follow us. So keep mum, everyone."

They all promised, and then they lent themselves to the task of getting things in shape for travel. Eradicate was a big help, and his cheerful good nature often lightened their toil.

At last all was in readiness, and with a caravan of six ox carts (for the balloon and its accessories took up much space) they started off, the Mexican drivers cracking their long whips, and singing their strange songs.

"Ho, for the interior!" cried Ned gaily.

"Yes, we're off into the unknown all right," added Tom grimly, "and there's no telling when we'll get back, if we ever will, should the head hunters get after us."

"Bless my collar and tie! Don't talk that way. It gives me the cold shivers!" protested Mr. Damon.

CHAPTER XIII

FOLLOWED

"WELL, this is something like it!" exclaimed Ned as he sat in front of the campfire, flourishing a sandwich in one hand, and in the other a tin cup of coffee.

"It sure is," agreed Tom. "But I say, old man, would you just as soon wave your coffee the other way? You're spilling it all over me."

"Excuse me!" laughed Ned. "I'll be more careful in the future. Mr. Damon will you have a little more of these fried beans—*tortillas* or *frijoles* or whatever these Mexicans call 'em. They're not bad. Pass your plate, Mr. Damon."

"Bless my eyelashes!" exclaimed the odd man. "Water, please, quick!" and he clapped his hand over his mouth.

"What's the matter?" demanded Tom.

"Too much red pepper! I wish these Mexicans wouldn't put so much of it in. Water!"

Mr. Damon hastily swallowed a cup of the liquid which Ned passed to him.

"I spects dat was my fault," put in Eradicate, who did the cooking for the three whites, while the Mexicans had their own. "I were just a little short ob some ob dem funny fried beans, an' I took some from ober dere," and the colored man nodded toward the Mexican campfire. "Den I puts some red pepper in 'em, an' I done guess somebody'd put some in afo' I done it."

"I should say they had!" exclaimed Mr. Damon, drinking more water. "I don't see how those fellows stand it," and he looked to where the Mexican ox drivers were eagerly devouring the highly-spiced food.

It was the second day of their trip into the interior, and they had halted for dinner near a little stream of good water that flowed over a grassy plain. So far their trip had been quite enjoyable. The ox teams were fresh and made good time, the drivers were capable and jolly, and there was plenty of food. Tom had brought along a supply especially for himself and his friends, for they did not relish the kind the Mexican drivers ate, though occasionally the gold-seekers indulged in some of the native dishes.

"This is lots of fun," Ned remarked again, when Mr. Damon had been sufficiently cooled off. "Don't you think so, Tom?"

"Indeed I do. I don't know how near we are

to the place we're looking for, nor even if we're going in the right direction, but I like this sort of life."

"How long Massa Tom, befo' dat gold——" began Eradicate.

"Hush!" interrupted the young inventor quickly, raising a hand of caution, and glancing toward the group of Mexicans. He hoped they had not heard the word the colored man so carelessly used, for it had been the agreed policy to keep the nature of their search a secret. But at the mention of "gold" Miguel Delazes, the head ox driver, looked up quickly, and sauntered over to where Tom and the others were seated on the grass. This Delazes was a Mexican labor contractor, and it was through him that Tom had hired the other men and the ox carts.

"Ah, senors!" exclaimed Delazes as he approached, "I fear you are going in the wrong direction to reach the gold mines. If I had known at the start——"

"We're not looking for gold mines!" interrupted Tom quickly. He did not like the greedy look in the eyes of Delazes, a look that flared out at the mention of gold—a look that was crafty and full of cunning.

"Not looking for gold mines!" the contractor repeated incredulously. "Surely I heard some one say something about gold," and he looked at Eradicate.

"Oh, you mustn't mind what Rad says," cried Tom laughing, and he directed a look of caution at the colored man. "Rad is always talking about gold; aren't you, Rad?"

"I 'spects I is, Massa Tom. I shore would laik t' find a gold mine, dat's what I would."

"I guess that's the case with all of us," put in Ned.

"Rad, get the things packed up," directed Tom quickly. "We've had enough to eat and I want to make a good distance before we camp for the night." He wanted to get the colored man busy so the Mexican would have no chance to further question him.

"Surely the senors are not going to start off again at once—immediately!" protested Delazes. "We have not yet taken the siesta—the noon-day sleep, and——"

"We're going to cut out the siestas on this trip," interposed Tom. "We don't want to stay here too long. We want to find some good ruins that we can study, and the sooner we find them the better."

"Ah, then it is but to study—to photograph ruined cities and get relics, that the senors came to Mexico?"

Once more that look of cunning came in the Mexican's eyes.

"That's about it," answered Tom shortly. He did not want to encourage too much familiarity on the part of the contractor. "So, no siestas if you please, Senor Delazes. We can all siesta to-night."

"Ah, you Americanos!" exclaimed the Mexican with a shrug of his shoulders. He stroked his shiny black moustache. "You are ever so on the alert! Always moving. Well, be it so, we will travel on—to the ruined city—if we can find one," and he gave Tom a look that the latter could not quite understand.

It was hot—very hot—but Tom noticed that about a mile farther on, the trail led into a thick jungle of trees, where it would be shady, and make the going more comfortable.

"We'll be all right when we get there," he said to the others.

It was not with very good grace that the Mexicans got their ox teams ready. They had not objected very much when, on the day before Tom had insisted on starting off right after the mid-day meal, but now when it seemed that it was going to be a settled policy to omit the siesta, or noon sleep, there was some grumbling.

"They may make trouble for us, Tom," said

Ned in a low voice. "Maybe you'd better give in to them."

"Not much!" exclaimed the young inventor. "If I do they'll want to sleep all the while, and we'll never get any where. We're going to keep on. They won't kick after the first few times, and if they try any funny business—well, we're well armed and they aren't," and he looked at his own rifle, and Ned's. Mr. Damon also carried one, and Eradicate had a large revolver which he said he preferred to a gun. Each of our white friends also carried an automatic pistol and plenty of ammunition.

"I took care not to let the Mexicans have any guns," Tom went on. "It isn't safe."

"I'll wager that they've got knives and revolvers tucked away somewhere in their clothes," spoke Ned.

"Bless my tackhammer!" cried Mr. Damon. "Why do you say such blood-curdling things, Ned? You make me shiver!"

In a little while they took up the trail again, the ox carts moving along toward the comparatively cool woods. Our friends had a cart to themselves, one fitted with padded seats, which somewhat made up for the absence of springs, and Eradicate was their driver. Tom had made this arrangement so they might talk among themselves without fear of being overheard by the Mexicans. At first Senor Delazes had suggested that one of his own drivers pilot Tom's cart, saying:

"I know what the senors fear—that their language may be listened to, but I assure you that this man understands no English, do you, Josef?" he asked the man in question, using the Spanish.

The man shook his head, but a quick look passed between him and his employer.

"Oh, I guess we'll let Rad drive," insisted Tom calmly, "it will remind him of his mule Boomerang that he left behind."

"As the senor will," Delazes had replied with a shrug of his shoulders, and he turned away. So it was that Tom, Ned and Mr. Damon, in their own cart, piloted by the colored man, were in the rear of the little cavalcade.

"Have you any idea where you are going, Tom?" asked Ned, after they had reached the shade, when it was not such a task to talk.

"Oh, I have a good general idea," replied the young inventor. "I've studied the map Mr. Illingway sent, and according to that the city of— well, you know the place we're looking for— lies somewhere between Tampico and Zacatecas, and which the plain of the ruined temple which used to be near the ancient city of Poltec, is about a hundred and fifty miles north of the city of

Mexico. So I'm heading for there, as near as I can tell. We ought to fetch it in about a week at this rate."

"And what are we to do when we get there?" inquired Mr. Damon. "If we keep on to that place where the images are to be found, with this rascally crew of Mexicans, there won't be much gold for us." He had spoken in low tones, though the nearest Mexican cart was some distance ahead.

"I don't intend to take them all the way with us," said Tom. "When I think we are somewhere near the temple plain I'm going to make the Mexican's go into camp. Then we'll put the balloon together and we four will go off in that. When we find what we're looking for we'll go back, pick up the Mexicans, and make for the coast."

"If the head-hunters let us," put in Ned grimly.

"Bless my nail file! There you go again!" cried Mr. Damon. "Positively, Ned, you get on my nerves."

"Yais, Massa Ned, an' *I* jest wish yo' wouldn't mention dem head gen'men no mo'," added Eradicate. "I can't drive straight when I hears yo' say dem words, an' goodness knows dese oxes is wusser t' drive dan mah mule Boomerang."

"All right I'll keep still," agreed Ned, and then he and Tom, together with Mr. Damon, studied the map, trying to decide whether or not they were on the proper trail.

They made a good distance that day, and went into camp that night near the foot of some low hills.

"It will be cooler traveling to-morrow," said Tom. "We will be up higher, and though we'll have to go slower on account of the up grade, it will be better for all of us."

They found the trail quite difficult the next day, as there were several big hills to climb. It was toward evening, and they were looking for a good place to camp for the night, when Delazes, who was riding in the first cart, was observed to jump down and hasten to the rear."

"I wonder what he wants?" spoke Tom, as he noted the approaching figure.

"Probably he's going to suggest that we take a few days' vacation," ventured Ned. "He doesn't like work."

"Senor," began Delazes addressing Tom, who called to Eradicate to bring his oxen to a halt, "are you aware that we are being followed?"

"Followed? What do you mean?" cried the young inventor, looking quickly around.

"Bless my watch chain!" gasped Mr. Damon. "Followed? By whom?" He, too, looked around, as did Ned, but the path behind them was deserted.

"When last we doubled on our own trail, to make the ascent of the big hill a little easier," went on the Mexican, "I saw, on the road below us, two ox carts, such as are hired out to prospectors or relic seekers like yourself. At first I thought nothing of it. That was early this morning. When we stopped for dinner, once more having to double, I had another view of the trail, I saw the same two carts. And now, when we are about to camp, the same two carts are there."

He pointed below, for the caravan was on quite an elevation now, and down on the faint trail, which was in plain view, for it wound up the mountain like a corkscrew, were two ox carts, moving slowly along.

"They are the same ones," went on Delazes, "and they have been following us all day—perhaps longer—though this is the first I have noted them."

"Followed!" murmured Tom. "I wonder——"

From his valise he took a small but powerful telescope. In the fast-fading light he focused it on the two ox carts. The next moment he uttered an exclamation of anger and dismay.

"Who is it?" asked Ned, though he was almost sure what the answer would be.

"Andy Foger and his father!" cried Tom. "I might have known they'd follow us—to learn ——" and then he stopped, for Senor Delazes was regarding him curiously.

CHAPTER XIV

A WEARY SEARCH

"ARE you sure it's them?" asked Ned.

"Bless my toothpick!" cried Mr. Damon. "It isn't possible, Tom?"

"Yes, it is," said the young inventor. "It's the Fogers all right. Take a look for yourself, Ned."

The other lad did, and confirmed his chum's news, and then Mr. Damon also made sure, by using the glass.

"No doubt of it," the odd man said. "But what are you going to do, Tom?"

Our hero thought for a moment. Then, once more, he looked steadfastly through the glass at the other carts. The occupants of them did not appear to know that they were under observation, and at that distance they could not have made out our friends without a telescope. Tom ascertained that the Fogers were not using one.

"Has Senor Swift any orders?" asked Delazes. "Who are these Fogers? Enemies of yours I take it. Why should they follow you merely to find a ruined city, that the ruins and relics may be studied?"

"Here are the orders," spoke Tom, a bit sharply, not answering the question. "We'll camp and have supper, and then we'll go on and make all the distance we can after dark."

"What, travel at night?" cried the Mexican, as if in horror at the suggestion.

"Yes; why not?" asked Tom calmly. "They can't see us after dark, and if we can strike off on another trail we may throw them off our track. Surely we'll travel after supper."

"But it will be night—dark—we never work after dark," protested Delazes.

"You're going to this time," declared Tom grimly.

"But the oxen—they are not used to it."

"Nothing like getting used to a thing," went on the young inventor. "They won't mind after a rest and a good feed. Besides, there is a moon to-night, and it will be plenty light enough. Tell the men, Senor Delazes."

"But they will protest. It is unheard of, and——"

"Send them to me," said Tom quickly. "There'll be double pay for night work. Send them to me."

"Ah, that is good, Senor Swift. Double pay!

I think the men will not object," and with a greedy look in his black eyes the Mexican contractor hastened to tell his men of the change of plans.

Tom took another look at the approaching Fogers. Their carts were slowly crawling up the trail, and as Tom could plainly see them, he made no doubt but that his caravan was also observed by Andy and his father.

"I guess that's the best plan to throw them off'" agreed Ned, when they were once more underway. "But how are you going to explain to Delazes, Tom, the reason the Fogers are following us? He'll get suspicious, I'm afraid."

"Let him. I'm not going to explain. He can think what he likes, I can't stop him. More than likely though, that he'll put it down to some crazy whim of us 'Americanos.' I hope he does. We can talk loudly, when he's around, about how we want to get historical relics, and the Fogers are after the same thing. There have been several expeditions down this way from rival colleges or museums after Aztec relics, and he may think we're one of them. For the golden images are historical relics all right," added Tom in a lower voice.

The Mexicans made no objections to continuing on after supper, once they learned of the

double pay, and a little later they went into camp.
A turn of the trial hid the Fogers from sight,
but Tom and his frends had no doubt but what
they were still following.

It was rather novel, traveling along by the
light of the brilliant moon, and the boys and Mr.
Damon thoroughly enjoyed it. Orders had been
given to proceed as quietly as possible, for they
did not want the Fogers to learn of the night trip.

"They may see us," Tom had said when they
were ready to start, "but we've got to take a
chance on that. If the trail divides, however, we
can lose them."

"It does separate, a little farther on," Delazes
had said.

"Good!" cried Tom, "then we'll fool our rival
relic hunters and our museum will get the benefit."
He said this quite loudly.

"Ah, then you want the relics for a museum?"
asked the Mexican contractor quickly.

"Yes, if they pay enough," replied Tom, and
he meant it, for he had no doubt that many
museums would be glad to get specimens of the
golden images.

Just as they were about to start off Tom had
swept the moonlit trail with his night-glass, but
there was no sign of the Fogers, though they may
have seen their rivals start off.

"Let her go!" ordered Tom, and they were once more underway.

It was about five miles to where the trail divided, and it was midnight when they got there, for the going was not easy.

"Now, which way." asked Delazes, as the caravan came to a halt. "To the left or right?"

"Let me see," mused Tom, trying to remember the map the African missionary had sent him. "Do these roads come together farther on?"

"No, but there is a cross trail about twenty miles ahead by which one can get from either of these trails to the other. "

"Good!" cried the young inventor. "Then we'll go to the right, and we can make our way back. But wait a minute. Send a couple of carts on the left trail for about two miles. We'll wait here until they come back."

"The senor is pleased to joke," remarked the Mexican quickly.

"I never was more earnest in all my life," replied Tom.

"What's the answer?" asked Ned.

"I want to fool the Fogers. If they see cart tracks on both roads they won't know which one we took. They may hit on the right one first shot, and again, they may go to the left until they come to the place where our two carts turn back. In that case we'll gain a little time."

"Good!" cried Ned. "I might have known you had a good reason, Tom."

"Send on two carts," ordered the young inventor, and now Delazes understood the reason for the strategy. He chuckled as he ordered two of the drivers to start off, and come back after covering a couple of miles.

It was rather dreary waiting there at the fork of the trail, and to beguile the time Tom ordered fires lighted and chocolate made. The men appreciated this, and were ready to start off again when their companions returned.

"There," announced Tom, when they were on the way once more, "I think we've given them something to think over at any rate. Now for a few more miles, and then we'll rest until morning."

All were glad enough when Tom decided to go into camp, and they slept later than usual the next morning. The trail was now of such a character that no one following them could be detected until quite close, so it was useless to worry over what the Fogers might do.

"We'll just make the best time we can, and trust to luck," Tom said.

They traveled on for two days more, and saw

nothing of the Fogers. Sometimes they would pass through Mexican villages where they would stop to eat, and Tom would make inquiries about the ancient city of Poltec and the plain of the ruined temple. In every case the Mexicans shook their heads. They had never heard of it. Long before this Tom had ascertained that neither Delazes nor any of his men knew the location of this plain nor had they ever heard of it.

"If there is such a place it must be far in—very far in," the contractor had said. "You will never find it."

"Oh, yes, I will," declared Tom.

But when a week passed, and he was no nearer it than at first even Tom began to get a little doubtful. They made inquiries at every place they stopped, of villagers, of town authorities, and even in some cases of the priests who obligingly went over their ancient church records for them. But there was no trace of the temple plain, and of course none of the city of gold.

Peasants, journeying along the road, parties of travelers, and often little bodies of soldiers were asked about the ruined temple, but always the answer was the same. They had never heard of it, nor of the head-hunters either.

"Well, I'm glad of the last," said Mr. Damon, looking apprehensively around, while Eradicate felt of his head to see if it was still fast on his shoulders.

It was a weary search, and when two weeks had passed even Tom had to admit that it was not as easy as it had seemed at first. As for the Mexicans, they kept on, spurred by the offer of good wages. Delazes watched Tom narrowly, for a sign or hint of what the party was really after, but the young inventor and his friends guarded their secret well.

"But I'm not going to give up!" cried Tom. "Our map may be wrong, and likely it is, but I'm sure we're near the spot, and I'm going to keep on. If we don't get some hint of it in a few days, though, I'll establish a camp, go up in the air and see what I can pick out from the balloon."

"That's the stuff!" cried Ned. "It will be a relief from these rough ox carts.

So for the next few days they doubled and re-doubled on their trail, criss-crossing back and forth, ever hoping to get some trace of the temple, which was near the entrance to the city of gold. In all that time nothing was seen of the Fogers.

"We'll try the balloon to-morrow," decided Tom, as they went into camp one night, after a weary day. Every one was tired enough to sleep soundly under the tents which were set up over the carts, in which beds were laid. It must have been about midnight when Tom, who felt a bit chilly (for the nights were cool in spite of the heat of the day), got up to look at the campfire. It was almost out so he went over to throw on some more logs.

As he did so he heard a noise as if something or somebody had leaped down out of a tree to the ground. A moment later, before he could toss on the sticks he had caught up, Tom was aware of two eyes of greenish brightness staring at him in the glow of the dying fire, and not ten feet away.

CHAPTER XV

THE GOLDEN IMAGE

FOR a moment the young inventor felt a cold chill run down his spine, and, while his hair did not actually "stand up" there was a queer sensation on his scalp as if the hairs *wanted* to stand on end, but couldn't quite manage it.

Involuntarily Tom started, and one of the sticks he held in his hand dropped to the ground. The green eyes shifted—they came nearer, and the lad heard a menacing growl. Then he knew it was some wild animal that had dropped down from a tree and was now confronting him, ready to spring on the instant.

Tom hardly knew what to do. He realized that if he moved it might precipitate an attack on him, and he found himself dimly wondering, as he stood there, what sort of an animal it was.

He had about come to the conclusion that it was something between a cougar and a mountain lion, and the next thought that came to him was a wonder whether any one else in the camp was awake, and would come to his rescue.

He half turned his head to look, when again there came that menacing growl, and the animal came a step nearer. Evidently every movement Tom made aroused the beast's antagonism, and made him more eager to come to the attack.

"I've got to keep my eyes on him," mused the lad. "I wonder if there's any truth in the old stories that you can subdue a wild beast with your eyes—by glaring at him. But whether that's so or not, I've got to do it—keep looking him in the face, for that's all I can do."

True, Tom held in his hand some light sticks, but if it came to a fight they would be useless. His gun was back in the tent, and as far as he could learn by listening there was not another soul in the camp awake.

Suddenly the fire, which had almost died out, flared up, as a dying blaze sometimes will, and in the bright glare the young inventor was able to see what sort of beast confronted him. He saw the tawny, yellow body, the twitching tail, the glaring eyes and the cruel teeth all too plainly, and he made up his mind that it was some species of the cougar family. Then the embers flared out and it was darker than before. But it was not so dark but what Tom could still see the glaring eyes.

"I've got to get away from him—scare him—or shoot him," the lad decided on the instant. "I'd like to bowl him over with a bullet, but how can I get my gun?"

He thought rapidly. The gun was in the tent back of him, near where he had been sleeping. It was fully loaded.

"I've got to get it," reflected Tom, and then he dropped the other sticks in his hand. Once more the beast growled and came a step nearer—soft, stealthy steps they were, too, making no sound on the ground.

Then Tom started to make a cautious retreat backwards, the while keeping his eyes focused on those of the beast. He made up his mind that he would give that "hypnotism" theory a trial, at any rate.

But at his first backward step the beast let out such a fierce growl, and came on with such a menacing leap that Tom stood still in very terror. The animal was now so close to him that a short jump would hurl the beast upon the lad.

"This won't do," thought Tom. "Every time I go back one step he comes on two, and it won't take him long to catch up to me. And then, too, he'll be in the tent in another minute, clawing Ned or Mr. Damon. What can I do? Oh, for a gun!"

He stood still, and this seemed to suit the animal, for it remained quiet. But it never took its eyes off Tom, and the switching tail, and the low growls now and then, plainly indicated that the beast was but waiting its time to leap and give the death blow.

Then an idea came to Tom. He remembered that he had once read that the human voice had a wonderful effect on wild animals. He would try it.

"And I'm not going to sing him any slumber song, either," mused Tom. "I'll start on a low tone to call for Ned, and gradually raise my voice until I wake him up. Then I'll tell Ned to draw a bead on the beast and plunk him while I hold his attention."

Tom lost no time in putting his plan into operation.

"Ned! Ned! Say, old man, wake up! I'm in trouble! There's a beast as big as a lion out here. Ned! Ned! Ned!"

Tom began in a low voice, but increased his tones with each word. At first the beast seemed uneasy, and then it stopped switching its tail and just glared at Tom.

"Ned! I say Ned! Wake up!"

Tom listened. All was silent within the tent.

"Ned! Oh, Ned!"

Louder this time, but still silence.

"Hey, Ned! Are you ever going to wake up!
Get your gun! Your gun! Shoot this beast!
Ned! Ned!"

Tom waited. It seemed as if the beast was
nearer to him. He called once more.

"Ned! Ned!" He was fairly shouting now.
Surely some one must hear him.

"What's that? What's the matter? Tom?
Where are you?"

It was Ned's voice—a sleepy voice—and it
came from the interior of the tent.

"Here!" called Tom. "Out in front—by the
fire—get your gun, and get him with the first
shot, or it's all up with yours truly."

"Get who with the first shot. Who are you
talking about?"

"This cougar! Hurry Ned, he's creeping
nearer!"

Tom heard a movement behind him. He dared
not turn his head, but he knew it was his chum.
Then he heard a gasp and he knew that Ned had
seen the beast. Then all Tom could do was to
wait. And it was not easy waiting. At any moment the beast might spring, and, as far as he was
concerned it would be all over.

Nearer and nearer crept the brute.   Again Tom felt that queer sensation down his spine.

"Hurry, Ned," he whispered.

"All right," came back the reassuring answer. There was a moment of silence.

Crack!   A sliver of flame cut the darkness. There was a report that sounded like a cannon, and it was followed by an unearthly scream.   Instinctively Tom leaped back as he saw the greenish eyes change color.

The young inventor felt a shower of dirt thrown over him by the claws of the dying cougar, and then he realized that he was safe.   He raced toward the tent, to be met by Ned, and the next instant the camp was in wild commotion.

"Bless my slippers!" cried Mr. Damon.   "What has happened.   Tell me at once?"

"Fo' de lob of chicken!" yelled Eradicate from a tent he had all to himself—the cook tent.

"Santa Maria!   Ten thousand confusions! What is it?" fairly screamed Delazes.

"Are you all right, Tom?" called Ned.

"Sure.   It was a good shot."

And then came explanations.   Wood was thrown on the fire, and as the Mexicans gathered around the blaze they saw, twitching in the death throes, a big cougar, or some animal allied to it. Neither Tom nor his friends had ever seen one just like it, and the Mexican name for it meant nothing to them. But it was dead, and Tom was saved and the way he grasped Ned's hand showed how grateful he was, even if he did not say much.

Soon the excitement died out, after Tom had related his experience, and though it was some time before he and the others got to sleep again, they did finally, and the camp was once more quiet.

An early start was made the next day, for Tom had reconsidered his determination to assemble the balloon and explore in that air craft. And the reason for his reconsideration was this:

They had not gone far on their journey before they met a solitary Mexican, and of him they asked the usual question about the plain of the temple.

He knew nothing, as might have been expected, but he stated that there was a large village not far distant in which dwelt many old Mexicans.

"They might know something," he said.

"It's worth trying," decided Tom. "I'll wait until to-morrow about the balloon. We can make the village by noon, I guess. Perhaps we can get a clew there."

But it was nearly night when the ox carts drew into the Mexican settlement, for there was an accident in the afternoon, one of the vehicles breaking down.

There were fires blazing in many places in the

village, which was one of the most primitive sort, when our friends entered. They were curiously watched as they drove through on their way to a good camping site beyond.

And here, once more, fate stepped in to aid Tom in his search for the city of gold.

As they were out of corn meal, and needed some for supper, Tom told Eradicate to stop at one of the larger houses to buy some. The lad followed the colored man into the building, which seemed to be used by several families.

"We'll be obliged to yo' all fo' some corn meal," began Eradicate, picking out an aged Mexican to whom he addressed his request.

"What is it?" asked the Mexican in Spanish.

Tom put the question in that language, and he was on the point of explaining that they were travelers, when he stopped midway, and stared at something on a rude shelf in the main room of the house.

"Look! Look, Ned!" whispered Tom.

"What is it?" asked his chum.

"On that shelf! That image! The image of gold! One just like the drawing Mr. Illingway sent from Africa! Ned, we're on the trail at last, for there is one of the small images from the city of gold!" and Tom, with a hand that trembled in spite of himself, pointed at the small, yellow figure.

CHAPTER XVI

THE MAP ON THE GOLD

NATURALLY, when Tom pointed at the golden image, the eyes of all the Mexicans in the room, as well as those of the friends of the young inventor, followed. For a moment there was silence and then the aged Mexican, whom Eradicate had asked for corn meal, rapidly uttered something in Spanish.

"Yes! Yes!" chorused his companions, and they followed this up, by crying aloud when he had said something else: "No! No!" Then there was confused talking, seemingly directed at Tom, who, though he had lowered his hand, continued to stare at the golden image.

"What in the world are they saying?" asked Ned, who only knew a little Spanish.

"I can't get on to all of it," explained Tom above the confusion. "Evidently they think we've come to take the image away from them and they are objecting."

"Offer to buy it then," suggested Ned.

"That's what I'm going to do," answered Tom, and once more addressing the aged Mexican, who seemed to be at the head of the household, Tom offered to purchase the relic which meant so much to him, agreeing to pay a large sum.

This seemd to create further confusion, and one of the women of the household hastily took down the little statute and was carrying it into an inner room, when Miguel Delazes came up. He looked into the open doorway, glanced about the room which was illuminated by several rude oil lamps, saw the looks of wonder and surprise on the faces of Tom and his companions, noted the excitement among the Mexicans, and then he caught sight of the golden image which the woman held.

"Ah!" exclaimed Delazes, and there was a world of meaning in his tone. His small dark eyes glittered. They roved from the image to Tom, and back to the little golden figure again. "Ah!" muttered the contractor. "And so the senor has found that for what he was searching? It *is* gold after all, but such gold as never I have seen before. So, the senor hopes to get many relics like that for his museum? So, is it not? Ah, ha! But that is worth coming many miles to get!"

Tom realized that if he did not act quickly Delazes might have his secret, and once it was known that Tom was seeking the buried city of gold, the Mexicans could never be shaken off his trail. He decided on a bold step.

"Look here, Senor Delazes," said the young inventor. "I had no more idea that golden image was here than you did. I would like to buy it, in fact I offered to, but they don't seem to want to sell it. If you can purchase it for me I'll pay *you* a good price for it."

"And doubtless the senor would like many more," suggested Delazes, with an open sneer.

"Doubtless the senor would!" snapped Tom. "Look here, Delazes, I'm here on business, to get all the relics I can —this kind or any other that I may fancy. You can think we're after buried treasure if you want to—I'm not going to take the trouble to contradict you. I hired you and your men for a certain purpose. But if you don't want to stay and let me and my friends run things, the sooner you tell me so the better. But I don't want any more of your underhand remarks. Understand?"

For a moment Delazes stared at Tom with snapping eyes, as though he would like to have attacked him. Then, knowing that Tom and his friends were well armed, and doubtless thinking that strategy was better than open force, he bowed, smiled in what he probably meant for a friendly fashion, and said:

"The senor is pleased to joke. Very well, I shall believe what I like. Meanwhile, does Senor Swift commission me to buy the image for him?"

Tom hesitated a moment. He feared he would be no match for the shrewd Mexican, and he wondered how much Delazes already knew. Then he decided on keeping up his end boldly, as that had seemed to have the best effect.

"You can have a try at buying the image after I have failed," he said. "I'll try my hand first."

"Very well," assented the contractor. The talk had been in English, and none of the Mexicans gave any signs of having understood it. Tom realized that he was playing a dangerous game, for naturally Delazes would privately tell the Mexicans to put so high a price on the statute as to prevent Tom from getting it and then the contractor would make his own terms.

But Tom decided that this was the only course, and he followed it.

"We'll stay here in the village for to-night," he went on. "Delazes, you and your men can make yourselves comfortable with any friends you may find here. We'll set up our tent as usual, after we get some corn meal for supper. I'll talk to them about the relic to-morrow. They seem to be afraid now."

"Very well," assented the contractor again, and then he said something in Spanish to the aged Mexican. What it was Tom could not catch, for Delazes spoke rapidly and seemed to use some colloquial, or slang phrases with which our hero was not familiar. The old Mexican assented by a nod, and then he brought out some corn meal which Eradicate took. The woman with the golden image had gone into an inner room.

"Bless my pocketbook!" exclaimed Mr. Damon, when he Tom, Ned and Eradicate were busy setting up their tent near a campfire just on the edge of the village. "This is most unexpected. What are you going to do, Tom?"

"I hardly know. I want to have a talk with whoever owns that image, to learn where they got it. One thing is sure, it proves that Mr. Illingway's information about the city of gold is correct."

"But it doesn't tell us where it is," said Ned.

"It must be somewhere around here," declared his chum. "Otherwise the image wouldn't be here."

"Bless my gaiters, that's so!" exclaimed the odd man.

"Not necessarily," insisted Ned. "Why one of

the images is away over in Africa, and this one may have been brought hundreds of miles from the underground city."

"I don't believe so," declared Tom. "We're somewhere in the neighborhood of the city, according to Mr. Illingway's map, I'm sure. That would be true, image or no image. But when you take the little gold statue into consideration it makes me positive that I'm near the end of the trail. I've just got to have a talk with those people to learn where the statue came from."

"Look out for Delazes," warned Ned.

"I intend to. As soon as I can, I'm going to leave him and his men behind and set off in the balloon. But first. I want to get an idea of where to head for. We must locate the plain on which stands the ruined temple."

"It's getting exciting," remarked Ned. "I wish——"

"Supper am serbed in de dinin' cah!" interrupted Eradicate with a laugh, as he imitated a Pullman porter.

"That's the best thing you could wish for," put in Tom gaily. "Come on, we'll have a good meal, a sleep, and then we'll be ready to play detectives again to-morrow."

They all slept soundly that night, though Tom had some idea of staying awake to see if Delazes paid any secret visits to the house where the golden image was kept. But he realized that the Mexican, if he wanted to, could easily find means to outwit him, so the young inventor decided to get all the rest he could and trust to chance to help him out.

His first visit after breakfast was to the house of the aged Mexican. The image was not in sight, though Tom and Ned and Mr. Damon looked eagerly around for it. There was a curious light in the eyes of the old man as Tom asked for the little statue of gold. Delazes was not in evidence. Tom had to conduct the conversation in Spanish, no particularly easy task for him, though he made out all right.

"Will you sell the image?" he asked.

"No sell," replied the Mexican quickly.

"Will you please let me look at it?"

The Mexican hesitated a moment, called a command to some one in the next room, and, a moment later the old woman shuffled in, bearing the wonderful golden image. Tom could not repress a little gasp of delight as he saw it at close range, for it was beautifully carved out of solid, yellow gold.

The woman set it on a rude table, and the young inventor, Ned and Mr. Damon drew near to look at the image more closely. It was the work of a master artist. The statue was about eight inches high, and showed a man, dressed in flowing robes, seated crosslegged on a sort of raised pedestal. On the head was a crown, many pointed and the face beneath it showed calm dignity like that of a superior being. In one extended hand was a round ball, with lines on it to show the shape of the earth, though only the two American continents appeared. In the other hand was what might be tables of stone, a book, or something to represent law-giving authority.

"How much?" asked Tom.

"No sell," was the monotonous answer.

"Five hundred dollars," offered our hero.

"No sell."

"One thousand dollars."

"No sell."

"Why is it so valuable to you?" Tom wanted to know.

"We have him for many years. Bad luck come if he go." Then the Mexican went on to explain that the image had been in his family for many generations, and that once, when it had been taken by an enemy, death and poverty followed until the statue was recovered. He said he would never part with it.

"Where did it come from?" asked Tom, and he

cared more about this than he did about buying
the image.

"Far, far off," said the Mexican. "No man
know. I no know—my father he no know—his
father's father no know. Too many years back
—many years."

He motioned to the woman to take the statue
away, and Tom and his friend realized that little
more could be learned. The young inventor
stretched out his hand with an involuntary motion, and the Mexican understood. He spoke to
the woman and she handed the image to Tom.
The Mexican had recognized his desire for a
moment's closer inspection and had granted it.

"Jove! It's as heavy as lead!" exclaimed Tom.
"And solid gold."

"Isn't it hollow up the middle?" asked Ned.
"Look on the underside, Tom."

His chum did so. As he turned the image
over to look at the base he had all he could do not
to utter a cry of surprise. For there, rudely
scratched on the plain surface of the gold, was
what was unmistakably a map. And it was a
map showing the location of the ruined temple—
the temple and the country surrounding it—the
ancient city of Poltec, and the map was plain
enough so that Tom could recognize part of the
route over which they had traveled.

But, better than all, was a tiny arrow, something like the compass mark on modern maps. And this arrow pointed straight at the ruins of the temple, and the direction indicated was due west from the village where our travelers now were. Tom Swift had found out what he wanted to know.

Without a word he handed back the image and then, trying not to let his elation show in his face, he motioned to Ned and Mr. Damon to follow him from the house.

"Bless my necktie!" exclaimed the odd man, when they were out of hearing distance. "What's up, Tom."

"I know the way to the ruined temple. We'll start at once," and he told them of the map on the image.

"Who do you suppose could have made it?" asked Ned.

"Probably whoever took the image from the city of gold. He wanted to find his way back again, or show some one, but evidently none of the recent owners of the image understand about the map, if they know it's there. The lines are quite faint, but it is perfectly plain.

"It's lucky I saw it. I don't have to try to buy the image now, nor seek to learn where it came from. Anyhow, if they told me they'd tell

Delazes, and he'd be hot after us. As it is I doubt if he can learn now. Come, we'll get ready to hit the trail again."

And they did, to the no small wonder of the contractor and his men, who could not understand why Tom should start out without the image, or without having learned where it came from, for Delazes had questioned the old Mexican, and learned all that took place. But he did not look on the base of the statue.

Due west went the cavalcade, and then a new complication arose. Tom did not want to take the Mexicans any nearer to the plain of the temple than possible, and he did not know how many miles it was away. So he decided on taking a longer balloon voyage than at first contemplated.

"We'll camp to-night at the best place we can find," he said to Delazes, "and then I'm going on in the balloon. You and your men will stay in camp until we come back."

"Ha! And suppose the senors do not come back with the balloon?"

"Wait a reasonable time for us, and then you can do as you wish. I'll pay you to the end of the month and if you wait for us any longer I have given instructions to the bank in Tampico to pay you and your men what is right."

"Good! And the senors are going into the unknown?"

"Yes, we don't know where we'll wind up. This hunting for relics is uncertain business. Make yourselves comfortable in camp, and wait.

"Waiting is weary business, Senor Swift. If we could come with you——" began Delazes, with an eager look in his eyes.

"Out of the question," spoke Tom shortly. "There isn't room in the balloon."

"Very well, senor," and with a snapping glance from his black eyes the contractor walked away.

CHAPTER XVII

THE RUINED TEMPLE

Though Tom had his portable balloon in shape for comparatively quick assembling it was several days, after they went into permanent camp, before it was in condition for use.

The Mexicans were not of much help for several reasons. Some of them were ignorant men, and were very superstitious, and would have nothing to do with the "Air Fiend" as they called it. In consequence Tom, Ned, Mr. Damon and Eradicate had to do most of the work. But Tom and Ned were a host in themselves, and Mr. Damon was a great help, though he often stopped to bless something, to the no small astonishment of the Mexicans, one of whom innocently asked Tom if this eccentric man was not "a sort of priest in his own country, for he called down so many blessings?"

"Bless my pen wiper!" exclaimed Mr. Damon, when Tom had told him. "I must break myself of that habit. Bless my——" and then he stopped and laughed, and went on with the work of help-ing to install the motor.

Another reason why some of the Mexicans were of little service was because they were so lazy. They preferred to sit in the shade and smoke innumerable cigarettes, or sleep. Then, too, some of them had to go out after some small game with which that part of the country abounded, for though there was plenty of tinned food, fresh meat was much more appreciated.

But Tom and Ned labored long and hard, and in about a week after making camp they had as-sembled the dirigible balloon in which they hoped to set out to locate the plain of the ruined temple, and also the entrance to the underground city of gold.

"Well, I'll start making the gas to-morrow," decided Tom, in their tent one night, after a hard day's work. "Then we'll give the balloon a try-out and see how she behaves in this part of the world. The motor is all right, we're sure of that much," for they had given the engine a test sev-eral days before.

"Which way are we going to head?" asked Ned.

"North, I think," answered Tom.

"But I thought you said that the temple was west——"

"Don't you see my game?" went on the young inventor quickly, and in a low voice, for several times of late he had surprised some of the Mexicans sneaking about the tent. "As soon as we start off Delazes is going to follow us."

"Follow us?" cried Mr. Damon. "Bless my shoe horn, what do you mean?"

"I mean that he still suspects that we are after gold, and he is going to do his best to get on our trail. Of course he can't follow us through the air, but he'll note in what direction we start and as soon as we are out of sight he and his men will hit the trail in the same direction."

"What, and leave the camp?" asked Ned.

"Yes, though they'll probably skip off with some of our supplies. That's why I'm going to take along an unusually large supply. We may not come back to this camp at all. In fact, it won't be much use after Delazes and his crowd clean it out and leave."

"And you really think they'll do that, Tom?" asked his chum.

"I'm almost sure of it, from the way the Mexicans have been acting lately. Delazes has been hinting around, trying to surprise me into saying which direction we're going to take. But I've been careful. The sight of that golden image aroused him and his men. They're hungry for gold, and they'd do away with us in a minute if they thought they could find what we're looking for and get it without us. But our secret is ours yet, I'm glad to say. If only the balloon behaves we ought soon to be in the——"

"Hark!" exclaimed Ned, holding up a warning hand. They heard a rustling outside the tent, and one side bulged in, as if some one was leaning against it.

"Some one's listening," whispered Ned.

Tom nodded. The next moment he drew his heavy automatic revolver and remarked in loud tones:

"My gun needs cleaning. I'm going to empty it through the tent where that bulge is—look out, Ned."

The bulge against the canvas disappeared as if by magic, and the sound of some one crawling or creeping away could be heard outside. Tom laughed.

"You see how it is," he said. "We can't even think aloud."

"Bless my collar button; who was it?" asked Mr. Damon.

"Some of Delazes's men—or himself," replied the young inventor. "But I guess I scared him."

"Maybe it was Andy Foger," suggested Ned with a smile.

"No, I guess we've lost track of him and his father," spoke Tom. "I've kept watch of the back trail as much as I could, and haven't seen them following us. Of course they may pick up our trail later and come here, and they may join forces with the Mexicans. But I don't know that they can bother us, once we're off in the balloon."

To Tom's disappointment, the next day proved stormy, a heavy rain falling, so it was impossible to test the balloon with the gas. The camp was a disconsolate and dreary place, and even Eradicate, usually so jolly, was cross and out of sorts.

For three days the rain kept up, and Tom and Ned thought they would never see the last of it, but on the fourth morning the sun shone, wet garments and shoes were dried out, tents were opened to the warm wind and everyone was in better spirits. Tom and his chum at once set about making gas for the big bag, their operations being closely watched by the Mexicans.

As I have explained before, Tom had the secret of making a very powerful gas from comparatively simple ingredients, and the machinery for this was not complicated. So powerful was it that the bag of the dirigible balloon did not need to be as large as usual, a distinct saving in space.

In a short time the bag began to distend and

then the balloon took shape and form. The bag was of the usual cigar shape, divided into many compartments so that the puncture of one would not empty out all the vapor.

Below the bag was a car or cabin made of light wood. It was all enclosed and contained besides the motor, storage tanks for gasolene, oil and other things, sleeping berths, a tiny kitchen, a pilot house, and a room to be used for a living apartment. Everything was very compact, and there was not half the room there was in some of Tom Swift's other airships. But then the party did not expect to make long voyages.

They could take along a good supply of canned and also compressed food, much of which was in tablet or capsule form, and of course they would take their weapons, and ammunition.

"And I hope you'll leave room for plenty of gold," said Ned in a whisper to Tom, as they completed arrangements for the gas test.

"I guess we can manage to store all that we can get out of the underground city," replied his chum. "I'm going to find a place for the big gold statue if we can manage to lift it."

"Say, we'll be millionaires all right!" exulted Ned.

Though much still remained to be done on the balloon, it was soon in shape for an efficient test,

and that afternoon Tom, Ned and Mr. Damon
went up in it to the no small wonder, fear and
delight of the Mexicans. Some, who had never
seen an air craft before, fell on their knees and
prayed. Others shouted, and when Tom started
the motor, and showed how he could control his
aircraft, there were yells of amazement.

"She'll do!" cried the young inventor, as he
let out some gas and came down.

Thereupon followed busy days, stocking the
airship for the trip to discover the ruined temple.
Food and supplies were put aboard, spare garments, all their weapons and ammunition, and
then Tom paid Delazes and his men, giving them
a month's wages in advance, for he told them
to wait in camp that long.

"But they won't," the young inventor predicted to Ned.

There was nothing more to be done. All that
they could do, to insure success had been completed. From now on they were in the hands of
fate.

"All aboard!" cried Tom, as he motioned for
Eradicate to take his place in the car. Mr. Damon
and Ned followed, and then the young inventor
himself. He shook hands with Delazes, though
he did not like the man.

"Good bye," said Tom. "We may be back before the month is up. If we are not, go back to Tampico."

"Si, senor," answered the contractor, bowing mockingly.

Tom turned the lever that sent more gas into the bag. The balloon shot up. The young gold-seeker was about to throw on the motor, when Delazes waved his hand to the little party.

"Bon voyage!" he called. "I hope you will find the city of gold!"

"Bless my soul!" cried Mr. Damon. "He knows our secret!"

"He's only guessing at it," replied Tom calmly. "He's welcome to follow us—if he can."

Up shot the aircraft, the propellers whirling around like blades of light. Up and up, higher and higher, and then forward, while down below the Mexicans yelled and swung their hats.

Straight for the north Tom headed his craft, so as to throw the eagerly watching ones off the track. He intended to circle around and go west when out of sight.

And then the very thing Tom had predicted came to pass. The balloon was scarcely half a mile high when, as the young inventor looked down, he uttered a cry.

"See!" he said. "They're breaking camp to follow us."

And it was so. Riding along in one of the lightest ox carts was Delazes, his eyes fixed on the balloon overhead, while behind him came his followers.

"They're following us," said Tom, "but they're going to get sadly left."

In an hour Tom knew his balloon would not be visible to the Mexicans, and at the end of that time he pointed for the west. And then, flying low so as to use the trees as a screen, but going at good speed, Tom and his friends were well on their way to the city of gold.

"We must keep a good lookout down below," said Tom, when everything was in working order. "We don't want to fly over the plain of the ruined temple."

"We may in the night," suggested Ned.

"No night flying this time," said his chum. "We'll only move along daytimes. We'll camp at night."

For three days they sailed along, sometimes over vast level plains on which grazed wild cattle, again over impenetrable jungles which they could never have gotten through in their ox carts. They crossed rivers and many small lakes, stopping each night on the ground, the airship securely anchored to trees. Tom could make the lifting gas on board so what was wasted by each descent was not missed.

One day it rained, and they did not fly, spending rather a lonely and miserable twelve hours in the car. Another time a powerful wind blew them many miles out of their course. But they got back on it, and kept flying to the west.

"We must strike it soon," murmured Tom one day.

"Maybe we're too far to the north or south," suggested Ned.

"Then we'll have to beat back and forth until we get right," was Tom's reply. "For I'm going to locate that ruined temple."

They ate breakfast and dinner high in the air, Eradicate preparing the meals in the tiny kitchen. Ever did they keep looking downward for a sight of a great plain, with a ruined temple in the midst of it.

In this way a week passed, the balloon beating back and forth to the North or South, and they were beginning to weary of the search, and even Tom, optimistic as he was, began to think he would never find what he sought.

It was toward the close of day, and the young inventor was looking for a good place to land. He was flying over a range of low hills, hoping the thick forest would soon come to an end when, as he crossed the last of the range of small mountains, he gave a cry, that drew the attention of Ned and Mr. Damon.

"What is it?" demanded his chum.

"Look!" said Tom. "There is the great plain!"

Ned gazed, and saw, spread out below them a vast level plateau. But this was not all he saw, for there, about in the centre, was a mass of something—something that showed white in the rays of the setting sun.

"Bless my chimney!" cried Mr. Damon. "That's some sort of a building."

"The ruined temple," said Tom softly. "We've found it at last," and he headed the balloon for it and put on full speed.

CHAPTER XVIII

FINDING THE TUNNEL

In silence, broken only by the noise of the motor, did the gold-seekers approach the temple. As they neared it they could see its vast proportions, and they noted that it was made of some white stone, something like marble. Then, too, as they drew closer, they could see the desolate ruin into which it had fallen.

"Looks as if a dynamite explosion had knocked it all apart," observed Ned.

"It certainly does," agreed Mr. Damon.

"Maybe Cortez, or some of those early explorers, blew it up with gunpowder after fighting the Aztecs, or whatever the natives were called in those days," suggested Tom.

"Bless my bookcase! You don't mean to say you think this temple goes back to those early days," spoke Mr. Damon.

"Yes, and probably farther," declared Tom. "It must be very ancient, and the whole country about here is desolate. Why, the way the woods have grown up everywhere but on this plain shows that it must be three or four hundred years ago. There must have been a city around the temple, probably Poltec, and yet there isn't a trace of it that we have seen as we came along. Oh, yes, this is very ancient."

"It will be jolly fun to explore it," decided Ned. "I wish it wasn't so near night."

"We can't do much now," decided Tom. "It will be too dark, and I don't altogether fancy going in those old ruins except by daylight."

"Do you think any of those old Aztec priests, with their knifes of glass, will sacrifice you on a stone altar?" asked Ned, with a laugh.

"No, but there might be wild beasts in there," went on the young inventor, "and I'm sure there are any number of bats. There must be lots of nooks and corners in there where a whole army could hide. It's an immense place."

The ruined temple certainly was large in extent, and in its glory must have been a wonderful place. The balloon came nearer, and then Tom let it sink to rest on the sand not far from the ancient ruin. Out he leaped, followed by his friends, and for a moment they stood in silent contemplation of the vast temple. Then as the last rays of the setting sun turned the white stones to gold, Tom exclaimed:

"A good omen! I'm sure the city of gold must be near here, and in the morning we'll begin our search for the secret tunnel that leads to it."

"That's the stuff!" cried Ned enthusiastically.

An instant later it seemed to get dark very suddenly, as it does in the tropics, and almost with the first shadows of night there came a strange sound from the ruined temple.

It was a low moaning, rumbling sound, like a mighty wind, afar off, and it sent a cold shiver down the spines of all in the little party.

"Good land a' massy! What am dat?" moaned Eradicate, as he darted back toward the balloon.

"Bless my looking glass!" cried Mr. Damon.

A second later the noise suddenly increased, and something black, accompanied by a noise of rapidly beating wings rushed from one of the immense doorways.

"Bats!" cried Tom. "Thousands of bats! I'm glad we didn't go in after dark!" And bats they were, that had made the noise as they rushed out on their nightly flight.

"Ugh!" shuddered Mr. Damon. "I detest the creatures! Let's get under cover."

"Yes," agreed Tom, "we'll have supper, turn in, and be up early to look for the tunnel. We're here at last. I'll dream of gold to-night."

Eradicate soon had a meal in preparation,

though he stopped every now and then to peer
out at the bats, that still came in unbroken flight
from the old temple. Truly there must have been
many thousands of them.

Whether Tom dreamed of gold that night he
did not say, but he was the first one up in the
morning, and Ned saw him hurrying over the
sands toward the temple.

"Hold on, Tom!" his chum called as he hastened to dress. "Where you going?"

"To have a hunt for that tunnel before breakfast. I don't want to lose any time. No telling
when Delazes and his crowd may be after us. And
the Fogers, too, may strike our trail. Come on,
we'll get busy."

"Where do you think the tunnel will be?"
asked Ned, when he had caught up to Tom.

"Well, according to all that Mr. Illingway
could tell us, it was somewhere near this temple.
We'll make a circle of it, and if we don't come
across it then we'll make another, and so on, increasing the size of the circles each time, until we
find what we're looking for."

"Let's have a look inside the temple first,"
suggested Ned. "It must have been a magnificent
place when it was new, and with the processions
of people and priests in their golden robes."

"You ought to have been an Aztec," suggested

Tom, as he headed for one of the big doorways.

They found the interior of the temple almost as badly in ruins as was the outside. In many places the roof had fallen in, the side walls contained many gaping holes, and the stone floor was broken away in many places, showing yawning, black caverns below. They saw hundreds of bats clinging to projections, but the ugly creatures were silent in sleep now.

"Bur-r-r-r-r!" murmured Ned. "I shouldn't like any of 'em to fall on me."

"No, it's not a very nice place to go in," agreed Tom.

They saw that the temple consisted of two parts, or two circular buildings, one within the other. Around the outer part were many rooms, which had evidently formed the living apartments of the priests. There were galleries, chambers, halls and assembly rooms. Then the whole of the interior of the temple, under a great dome that had mostly fallen in, consisted of a vast room, which was probably where the worship went on. For, even without going farther than to the edge of it, the youths could see stone altars, and many strangely-carved figures and statues. Some had fallen over and lay in ruins on the floor. The whole scene was one of desolation.

"Come on," invited Tom, "it's healthier and

more pleasant outside. Let's look for that tunnel."

But the lads soon realized that it was not going to be as easy to locate this as they had hoped. They were looking for some sort of slanting opening, going down into the earth—the entrance to the underground city—but though they both made a complete circuit of the temple, each at a varying distance from the outer walls, no tunnel entrance showed.

"Breakfast! Breakfast!" called Eradicate, when Tom was about to start on a second round.

"Let's eat," suggested Ned, "and then we four can circle around together." Tom agreed that this would be a good plan. A little later then, with Tom nearest the temple walls, the four began their march around them.

Four times that morning they made the circuit, and the same number in the afternoon, until they were nearly half a mile away from the ruin, but no tunnel showed.

"Well, we'll have to keep at it to-morrow," suggested Tom. "It's too soon to give up."

But the morrow brought no better success, nor did the following two days. In fact for a week they kept up the search for the tunnel, but did not come upon it, and they had now pretty well covered the big plain. They found a few ruins of the ancient city of Poltec.

"Well, what about it?" asked Ned one night as they sat in the balloon, talking it over. "What next, Tom?"

"We've got to keep at it, that's all. I think we'll go up in the balloon, circle around over the plain at just a little elevation, and maybe we can spot it that way."

"All right, I'm with you."

But they did not try that plan. For in the middle of the night Ned suddenly awakened. Something had come to him in his sleep.

"Tom! Tom!" he cried. "I have it! What chumps we were!"

"What's the matter, old man?" asked Tom anxiously. "Are you sick—talking in your sleep?"

"Sleep nothing! I've just thought of it. That tunnel entrance is *inside* the temple. That's the most natural place in the world for it. I'll bet it's right in the middle of the big inner chamber, where the priests could control it. Why didn't we look there before?"

"That's right; why didn't we?" agreed Tom. "I believe you're right, Ned! We'll look the first thing in the morning."

They did not wait for breakfast before trying

the experiment, and Mr. Damon and Eradicate
went with Tom and Ned. It was no easy work
to make their way over the ruins to the inner
auditorium. Wreckage and ruin was all around,
and they had to avoid the yawning holes on every
side. But when they got to the main, or sacrificial
chamber, as Ned insisted on calling it, they found
the floor there solid. In the centre was a great
altar, but to their chagrin there was not a sign of
a tunnel opening.

"Fooled again!" said Tom bitterly.

"Maybe some of those holes outside is the entrance," suggested Mr. Damon.

"I don't believe so," objected Tom. "They
seemed to go only to the cellar, if a temple has
such a thing."

Bitterly disappointed, Tom strolled over and
stood in front of the big stone altar. It seemed
that he must give up the search. Idly he looked
at the sacrificial stone. Projecting from it was
a sort of a handle.

Tom took hold of it, and to his surprise he
found that it could be moved. Hardly knowing
what he was doing, he pulled it toward him.

The next instant he uttered a cry of horror,
for the immense stone altar, with a dull rumbling,
rolled back as though on wheels, and there, over
where it had stood was a hole of yawning black-

ness, with a flight of stone steps leading down into it. And Tom stood so near the edge that he almost toppled in.

"Look! Look!" he cried when he could get his gasping breath, and step back out of danger.

"The tunnel entrance!" cried Ned. "That's what it is! You've found it, Tom! The entrance to the city of gold at last!"

CHAPTER XIX

THE UNDERGROUND RIVER

THEY gathered around the opening so unexpectedly disclosed to them, and stared down into the black depths. Beyond the first few steps of the flight that led to they knew not where, nothing could be seen. In his impatience Tom was about to go down.

"Bless my match box!" cried Mr. Damon. "What are you going to do, Tom, my boy?"

"Go down there, of course! What else? I want to get to the underground city."

"Don't!" quickly advised the odd man. "You don't know what's there. It may be a trap, where the old Aztecs used to throw their victims. There may be worse things than bats there. You'll need torches—lights—and you'd better wait until the air clears. It may have been centuries since that place was opened."

"I believe that's right," agreed Ned. "Whew! Smell it! It's as musty as time!"

An unpleasant odor came up the tunnel entrance, and it was stifling to stand too close. Tom lighted a match and threw it down. Almost instantly the flame was snuffed out.

"We couldn't live down there a minute," said the young inventor. "We've got to wait for it to clear. We'll go back to the balloon and get some electric flash lamps. I brought along a lot of 'em, with extra strong batteries. I thought we'd need some if we did find the city of gold, and it looks as if we were almost there now."

Tom's plan was voted good so they hurried out of the temple, their feet echoing and re-echoing over the stone floor. The place, ruined and desolate as it was, had no terrors for them now. In fact they were glad of the very loneliness, and Tom and Ned actually looked about apprehensively as they emerged, fearing they might see a sign of the Mexicans or the Fogers.

"Guess they can't pick up our trail," said Tom, when he saw of what Ned was thinking.

"No, we've got the place to ourselves. I wonder how long it will take for the air to get fresh?"

"Not so very long, I guess. There was a good draught. There must be some opening in the underground city by which the air is sucked in. They'd never have only one opening to it. But we don't need to look for the other. Come on, we'll get out the torches."

These electrical contrivances are familiar to all boys. A small electric lamp is set in the end of a hollow tube of tin, and about the lamp is a reflector. Dry electrical batteries are put in the tin tube, and by means of a push button the circuit is closed, illuminating the lamp, which gives a brilliant glow. Tom had a special kind of lamp, with tungsten filaments, which gave a very powerful light, and with batteries designed to last a long time. A clip on the spring controlling the push button made it so that the lamp could be made to give a steady glow. Thus they were well prepared for exploring the tunnel.

It took some little time to get the flash lamps ready, and when they were all charged and they had eaten, they went back to the opening to see if the air had cleared. Tom tested it by dropping a match down, and, to his delight it burned with a clear flame.

"It's all right!" he exclaimed. "The air is pure. Now to see where we will bring up. Come on, everybody."

"Jest one minute, Massa Tom," begged Eradicate, as the young inventor was about to descend the steps, which even the brightness of his lamp did not disclose the end. "Is yo' gwine down dar, Massa Tom?"

"Certainly, Rad."

"An' is yo'—'scuse me—but is yo' expectin'
me fo' t' follow yo'?"

"Certainly, Rad."

"Den, all I's got t' say is dat yo' is 'spectin'
too much. I ain't gwine t' bury mahse'f alive
not yit."

"But, Rad, this is where the gold images are.
If you don't come down with us you won't get
any gold."

"Am dat so? No gold?" The colored man
scratched his head. "Well, I shore does want
gold," he murmured. "I reckon I'd better trot
along. But one thing mo', Massa Tom."

"What is it, Rad?"

"Was yo' all aimin' t' stay down thar any
length ob time? 'Case if yo' is yo' all'd better
take along a snack ob suffin' t' eat. 'Case when
I gits among gold I don't want t' come out very
soon, an' we might stay dar all day."

"Good advice, Rad," exclaimed Ned with a
laugh. "I think we may get hungry. You go
back and put us up a lunch. We'll wait for you."

"Bless my napkin ring! I think you're right!"
exclaimed Mr. Damon, and Eradicate hurried
back to the balloon to get some of the condensed
food.

He was soon back and then, with Tom in the
lead, and with everyone carrying an electric torch,

with a spare one in reserve, and with their weapons in readiness the party descended the stone steps.

Their footfalls echoed solemnly as they went down—down into the unknown blackness. They kept their bright lights playing here and there, but even these did not dispell the gloom. On every side was stone—stone walls—stone steps. It was like going down into some vast stretch of catacombs.

"Say, will we ever get to the bottom?" asked Ned, when they had counted several hundred steps. "Maybe this goes down to the middle of the earth."

"Well, ef it do I'm gwine right along!" called Eradicate. "I's gwine t' hab one ob dem gold images er bust!"

"And I'm with you!" cried Tom. "We'll have to get to the bottom sooner or later."

Hardly had he spoken than he came to the last step, and saw stretching off before him a long tunnel, straight and level, lined on both sides, and top and bottom, with smooth stones that gleamed like marble.

"Now we are really in the tunnel," declared Ned. "I wonder what's at the end?"

"The city of gold, of course," answered Tom confidently.

Eagerly they hurried on. There was a slightly

musty smell to the air, but it was fresher than might have been expected.

Suddenly Tom, who was in advance, uttered a cry. It sounded like one of alarm, and Ned yelled:

"What's the matter?"

"Look here!" cried Tom. They hurried up to him, to find him standing before a sort of niche in the wall. And the niche was lined with a yellow metal that gleamed like gold, while in it was one of the golden images, the second one they had seen, and the third they heard about.

"We're on the trail! We're on the trail!" cried Tom.

"Heah! Let me hab dat!" cried Eradicate. "I may not git anudder," and he reached up for the statue.

"Let it stay until we come back," suggested Mr. Damon.

"Somebody might take it," said the colored man.

"Who?" laughed Tom. "There's not a soul here but ourselves. But take it, if you want it, Rad," and Eradicate did so, stuffing the image, which was only about four inches high, into his pocket.

Then they went on, and they saw several other images, though not of gold. Several niches were lined with yellow metal, but whether it was gold or not they could not tell. They did not want to stop, as they were anxious to get to the underground city.

"Hark! What's that?" asked Tom, when they had gone about a mile along the tunnel. "Don't you hear something?"

"Sounds like a roaring," agreed Ned. "Maybe it's more of the bats."

"Doesn't sound like bats," declared Tom. "It's more like a waterfall. Come on."

They hurried forward, the strange sound increasing at every step, until it filled the tunnel with its menacing roar.

"That's strange," said Tom in worried tones. "I hope we don't come to a waterfall."

Suddenly the tunnel made a turn, and as they went around the curve in the wall the sound smote on their ears with increased violence. Tom raced forward, focusing his electric lamp down on the stone corridor. The next instant he cried out:

"A river! It's an underground river and we can't go any further! We're blocked!"

The others came to his side, and there, in the glare of their lamps, they saw rushing along, between two walls of stone, a dark stream which caused the roaring sound that had come to them. The tunnel was cut squarely in two by the stream, which was at least thirty feet wide, and how deep they could only guess. Swiftly it flowed on, its roar filling the tunnel.

CHAPTER XX

THE CITY OF GOLD

"WELL, I guess this is the end of it," remarked Ned ruefully, as they stood contemplating the roaring stream by the gleam of their electric flash lamps. "We can't go on to the city of gold unless we swim that river, and——"

"And none of us is going to try that!" interrupted Tom sharply. "The strongest swimmer in the world couldn't make a yard against that current. He'd be carried down, no one knows where."

"Bless my bathing suit, yes!" exclaimed Mr. Damon. "But what are we to do? Can't we make a raft, or get a boat, or something like that?"

"Hab t' be a mighty pow'ful boat t' git across dat ribber ob Jordan," spoke Eradicate solemnly.

"That's right," agreed Ned. "But say, Tom, don't you think we could go back, get a lot of trees, wood and stuff and make some sort of a bridge? It isn't so very wide—not more than thirty or forty feet. We ought to be able to bridge it."

"I'm afraid not," and Tom shook his head. "In the first place any trees that would be long enough are away at the far edge of the big plain, and we'd have a hard job getting them to the temple, to say nothing of lugging them down the tunnel. Then, too, we don't know much about building a bridge, and with no one on the other side to help us, we'd have our hands full. One slip and we might be all drowned. No, I guess we've got to go back," and Tom spoke regretfully. "It's hard luck, but we've got to give up and go back."

"Den I's pow'ful glad I got ma golden image when I did, dat's suah!" exclaimed Eradicate. "Ef we doan't git no mo' I'll hab one. But I'll sell it an' whack up wid yo' all, Massa Tom."

"You'll do nothing of the sort, Rad!" exclaimed the young inventor. "That image is yours, and I'm sorry we can't get more of them."

He turned aside, and after another glance at the black underground river which flowed along so relentlessly he prepared to retrace his steps along the tunnel.

"Say, look here!" suddenly exclaimed Ned. "I'm not so sure, after all that we've got to turn back. I think we can go on to the city of gold, after all."

"How do you mean?" asked Tom quickly. "Do you think we can bring the balloon down here and float across?"

"Bless my watch chain!" exclaimed Mr. Damon, "but that *would* be a way. I wonder——"

"No, I don't mean that way at all," went on Ned. "But it seems to me as if this river isn't a natural one—I mean that it flows along banks of smooth stone, just as if they were cut for it, a canal you know."

"That's right," said Tom, as he looked at the edge of the channel of the underground stream. "These stones are cut as cleanly as the rest of the tunnel. Whoever built that must have made a regular channel for this river to flow in. And it's square on the other side, too," he added, flashing his lamp across.

"Then don't you see," continued Ned, "that this river hasn't always been here."

"Bless my gaiters!" gasped Mr. Damon, "what does he mean? The river not always been here?"

"No," proceeded Tom's chum. "For the ancients couldn't have cut the channel out of stone, or made it by cementing separate stones together while the water was here. The channel must have been dry at one time, and when it was finished they turned the water in it."

"But how is that going to help us?" asked Tom. "I grant you that the river may not have been here at one time, but it's here *now,* which makes it all the worse for us."

"But, Tom!" cried his chum, "if the river was turned aside from this channel once it can be done again. My notion is that the ancients could make the river flow here or not, just as they choose. Probably they turned it into this channel to keep their enemies from crossing to the city of gold, like the ancient moats. Now if we could only find——"

"I see! I see!" cried Tom enthusiastically. "You mean there must be some way of shutting off the water."

"Exactly," replied his chum. "We've got to shut that stream of water off, or turn it into some other channel, then we can cross, and keep on to the city of gold. And I think there must be some valve—some lever, or handle or something similar to the one that moved the altar—near here, that does the trick. Let's all look for it."

"Bless my chopping block!" cried Mr. Damon. "That's the strangest thing I ever heard of! But I believe you're right, Ned. We'll look for the handle to the river," and he laughed gaily.

Every one was in better spirits, now that there seemed a way out of the difficulty, and a moment later they were eagerly flashing their lamps on the sides, floor and ceiling of the tunnel, to discover the means of shutting off the water. At first they feared that, after all, Ned's ingenious theory was not to be confirmed. The walls, ceiling and floor were as smooth near the edge of the river as elsewhere.

But Eradicate, who was searching as eagerly as the others, went back a little, flashing his lamp on every square of stone. Suddenly he uttered a cry.

"Look yeah, Massa Tom! Heah's suffin' dat looks laik a big door knob. Maybe yo' kin push it or pull it."

They rushed to where he was standing in front of a niche similiar to the one where he had found the golden image. Sunken in the wall was a round black stone. For a moment Tom looked at it, and then he said solemnly:

"Well, here goes. It may shut off the water, or it may make it rise higher and drown us all, or the whole tunnel may cave in, but I'm going to risk it. Hold hard, everybody!"

Slowly Tom put forth his hand and pushed the knob of stone. It did not move. Then he pulled it. The result was the same—nothing.

"Guess it doesn't work any more," he said in a low tone.

"Twist it!" cried Ned. "Twist it like a door knob."

In a flash Tom did so. For a moment no result was apparent, then, from somewhere far off, there sounded a low rumble, above the roar of the black stream.

"Something happened!" cried Mr. Damon.

"Back to the river!" shouted Tom, for they were some distance away from it now. "If it's rising we may have a chance to escape."

They hurried to the edge of the stone channel, and Ned uttered a cry of delight.

"It's going down!" he yelled, capering about. "Now we can go on!"

And, surely enough, the river was falling rapidly. It no longer roared, and it was flowing more slowly.

"The water is shut off," remarked Tom.

"Yes, and see, there are steps which lead across the channel," spoke Ned, pointing to them as the receding water revealed them. "Everything is coming our way now."

In a short time the water was all out of the channel, and they could see that it was about twenty feet deep. Truly it would have been a formidable stream to attempt to swim over, but now it had completely vanished, merely a few little pools of water remaining in depressions on the bottom of the channel. There were steps leading down to the bottom, and other steps ascending on the other side, showing that the river was used as a barrier to further progress along the tunnel.

"Forward!" cried Tom gaily, and they went on.

They went down into the river channel, taking care not to slip on the wet steps, and a few seconds later they had again ascended to the tunnel, pressing eagerly on.

Straight and true the tunnel ran through the darkness, the only illumination being their electric flash lamps. On and on they went, hoping every minute to reach their goal.

"Dish suah am a mighty long tunnel," remarked Eradicate. "Dey ought t' hab a trolley line in yeah."

"Bless my punching bag!" cried Mr. Damon, "so they had! Now if those ancients were building to-day——"

He stopped suddenly, for Tom, who was in the lead, had uttered a cry. It was a cry of joy, there was no mistaking that, and instinctively they all knew that he had found what he had sought.

All confirmed it a moment later, for, as they

rushed forward, they discovered Tom standing at the place where the tunnel broadened out—broadened out into a great cave, a cave miles in extent, for all they could tell, as their lamps, powerful as they were, only illuminated for a comparatively short distance.

"We're here!" cried Tom. "In the city of gold at last!"

"The city of gold!" added Ned. "The underground city of gold!"

"And gold there is!" fairly shouted Mr. Damon. "See it's all over! Look at the golden streets—even the sides of the buildings are plated with it—and see, in that house there are even gold chairs! Boys, there is untold wealth here!"

"An' would yo' all look at dem golden statues!" cried Eradicate, "dey mus' be millions ob 'em! Oh, golly! Ain't I glad I comed along!" and he rushed into one of the many houses extending along the street of the golden city where they stood, and gathered up a fairly large statue of gold—an image exactly similiar to the one he already had, except as to size.

"I never would have believed it possible!" gasped Tom. "It's a city of almost solid gold. We'll be millionaires a million times over!"

CHAPTER XXI

THE BIG IMAGE

COULD the light of day have penetrated to that mysterious and ancient underground city of gold our friends might have had some idea of its magnificence. As it was they could only view small parts of it at a time by the illumination of their electric torches. But even with them they saw that it was a most wonderful place.

"I don't believe there's another city like it in all the world," spoke Tom in awed accents, "there never was, and never will be again. Those Aztecs must have brought all their treasures of gold here."

"Bless my cake box! that's so," agreed Mr. Damon.

"Let's take a look around," advised Ned, "and then we can decide on what will be best to take away."

"It won't take me long t' make up mah mind," spoke Eradicate. "I's goin' t' take all dem images I kin find."

"I was going to say we'd have plenty of time to look about and pick what we wanted," said Tom, "but I think perhaps we'd better hurry."

"Why?" asked Mr. Damon.

"There's no telling when Delazes and his gang may find this place, and even the Fogers may be nearer than we think. But I believe our best plan would be this: To take some gold now, and several of the statues, go back to our balloon, and make some kind of big lamps, so we can light this place up. Then, too, I think we'd better move the balloon into the old temple. It will be safer there. Then we can come back here, pack up as much gold as we can carry, and be off. I don't like to think of being underground when Delazes and the the Fogers are on the surface. It might not be altogether safe for us."

"Bless my insurance policy!" cried the odd man. "Now *you're* giving me the cold shivers, Tom. But I believe you're right. We must look ahead a bit."

With all their electric flash lamps turned on, the four advanced farther into the underground city of gold. As they went on they saw the precious yellow metal on every side of them. It was used lavishly, showing that to the ancients it was as common as iron or steel is to-day. But they did not use the gold merely as common material in the construction of buildings or objects of use. Instead, the gold seemed to be brought into play to beautify the city. An artistic scheme was carried out, and while it was true that in many buildings common objects were made of gold, yet each one was beautiful in itself.

"What a wonderful place this must have been when it was lighted up," spoke Tom.

"Do you think it was ever lighted up?" asked his chum.

"It must have been," declared the young inventor. "My idea is that this city was the home of the priests of the temple, and their friends. I don't believe the common people ever came here. Perhaps the officers of the army, the rulers and the royal family were admitted, but not the ordinary people. That's why it's so far underground, and so well guarded by the river.

"Probably the priests and others collected so much gold they didn't know what to do with it, and built this city to use it up, and, at the same time have a safe place to store it. And they must have had some means of lighting the place, for they couldn't go about in darkness—they couldn't have seen the gold if they did. Yes, this must have been wonderfully beautiful then. The priests probably came here to study, or perhaps to carry out some of their rites. Of course it's only guesswork, but it seems true to me."

"I believe you're right, Tom," said Mr. Damon.

As our friends walked about they saw that the city, while smaller than they had at first supposed, was laid out with regular streets. Each one was straight, and at certain places in the stone pavement plates of gold were set, so that literally the streets were paved with gold. There were houses or buildings on each side of the streets, and most of these were open at the doors or windows, for there was no need of heat in that buried city.

All about were the golden images such as they had seen in the Mexican's house, and like the one in far off Africa. Some of the images were almost life size, and others were only an inch or two inches in height. Not a house but had half a dozen or more in various places, and there were also the images on golden pedestals about the streets.

"This must have been their chief god, or else a representation of some great personage to whom they paid the highest honor," said Mr. Damon. "Perhaps he was the reigning king or ruler, and he, himself, might have ordered the images made out of vanity, like some men of to-day."

The boys agreed that this was a natural theory. As for Eradicate he was busy collecting numbers of the small golden statues, and stuffing them in his pockets.

"Why don't you take bigger ones, and not so many of them?" asked Tom.

" 'Case as how I doan't want all mah eggs in one basket," replied the colored man. "I kin carry mo' ob de little fellers," and he persisted in this plan.

They found in some of the houses utensils of solid gold, but there appeared to be no way of cooking food, and that was probably done outside, or in the great temple. In many houses were articles evidently used in the sacrificial rites or in worship of strange gods. They did not stay to half examine the wonderful city of gold, for it would have taken several days. But on Tom's advice, they took up a considerable quantity of the precious metal in the most convenient form to carry, including a number of the statues and art objects and started back along the tunnel.

"We'll rig up some sort of lamps," Tom explained, "and come back to make a thorough examination of this place. I think the scientific men and historians will be glad to know about this city, and I'm going to make some notes about it."

They soon came again to the place of the underground river and found no water there. Ned wanted to turn the stream back into the channel again, but Tom said they might not be able to work the ancient mechanism, so they left the black knob as it was, and hurried on. They decided that the knob must have worked some counter-balance, or great weight that let down a gate and cut off the river from one channel, to turn it into another.

When they emerged at the top af the steps, and came out at the opening which had been revealed by the rolling back of the great altar, they saw there that counter weights, delicately balanced, had moved the big stone.

"We might close that opening," said Tom, "and then if any one *should* come along and surprise us, they wouldn't know how to get to the underground city." This was done, the altar rolling back over the staircase.

"Now to get the balloon in the temple, make the lamps, and go back," suggested Tom, and, storing the gold they had secured in a safe place in the temple, they went back to move the airship.

This was an easy matter, and soon they had floated the big gas bag and car in through one of the immense doorways and so into the great middle part of the temple where the big stone altar was located.

"Now we're prepared for emergencies," remarked Tom, as he looked up at the yawning hole in the dome-like roof. "If worst comes to worst, and we have to run, we can float right up here, out of the temple, and skip."

"Do you think anything is going to happen?" asked Mr. Damon anxiously.

"You never can tell," replied Tom. "Now to make some lamps. I think I'll use gas, as I've got plenty of the chemicals."

It took two days to construct them, and Tom ingeniously made them out of some empty tins that had contained meat and other foods. The tins were converted into tanks, and from each one rose a short piece of pipe that ended in a gas tip. On board the dirigible were plenty of tools and materials. Into the cans were put certain chemicals that generated a gas which, when lighted, gave a brilliant glow, almost like calcium carbide.

"Now, I guess we can see to make our way about," remarked Tom, on the morning of the third day, whey they prepared to go back to the city of gold. "And we'll take plenty of lunch along, for we may stay until nearly night."

It did not take them long to roll back the altar, descend into the tunnel, and reach the underground city. The river channel was now dry, even the small pools of water in the depressions having evaporated.

The gas torches worked to perfection, and revealed the beauties and wonders of the city of gold to the astonished gaze of our friends. It was even richer in the precious metal than they had at first supposed.

"Before we do any exploring, I think we'd better take some more gold back to the balloon," suggested Tom, "and I think I'll just move the balloon itself more out of sight, so that if any persons come along, and look into the temple, they won't see our airship without looking for it."

This was done, and a considerable quantity of the precious metal, including a number of the larger-sized statues, were stored in the balloon car.

"We can't take much more," Tom warned his friends, "or we'll be over-weighted."

"We've got enough now, to make us all rich," said Ned, contentedly.

"I want moah," spoke Eradicate with a grin.

They went back to the underground city and began to explore it with a view of taking back to civilization some word of its wonders and beauties.

"Didn't Mr. Illingway, in his letters, say something about an immense golden statue here?" asked Ned, when they had almost completed a circuit of the underground place.

"So he did!" exclaimed Tom. "I'd almost forgotten. It must be somewhere in the centre of this place I should think. Let's have a hunt for it. We can't take it with us, but maybe we could get part of an arm or a leg to keep as a relic. Come on."

It was easy to reach the centre of the underground city, for it was laid out on a regular plan. In a short time they were in sight of the central plaza and, even before they reached it the glare of their gas lamps showed them something glittering golden yellow. It was on a tall, golden pedestal.

"There it is!" cried Ned.

"Yes, there's the big golden image all right," agreed Tom, hurrying forward, and a moment later they stood before a most wonderful statue.

CHAPTER XXII

TRAPPED

"WELL, that sure is a big statue!" exclaimed Ned as he walked around it.

"An' to t'ink dat it's *solid gold!*" cried Eradicate his eyes big with wonder. "I suah wish I had dat all fo' mahse'f!"

"We never could carry that in the balloon," spoke Tom with a shake of his head. "I guess we'll have to leave it here. But I would like to take say the head. It would be worth a lot as a relic to some museum—worth more than the value of the gold itself. I've a notion to do it."

"How could you get the head off?" asked Mr. Damon.

"Oh, pull the statue down or overturn it, as the American patriots did to the Bowling Green, New York, lead statue of King George III during the Revolutionary days," answered Tom. "I think that's what I'll do."

"I say, look here!" called Ned, who had made a circuit of the statue. "There's some sort of an inscription here. See if you can read it, Tom."

They went around to the front of the big, golden image where Ned stood. On a sort of a plate, with raised letters, was an inscription in a strange language. Part of it seemed to be the name of the person or god whom the statue represented, and what followed none could make out.

"It's something like the ancient Greek or Persian language," declared Mr. Damon, who was quite a scholar. "I can make out a word here and there, and it seems to be a warning against disturbing the statue, or damaging it. Probably it was put there to warn small boys thousands of years ago, if they ever allowed small boys in this place."

"Does it say what will be done to whoever harms the statue?" asked Tom with a laugh.

"Probably it does, but I can't make out what it is," answered Mr. Damon.

"Then here goes to see if we can't overturn it and hack off the head," went on Tom. "I've got a sharp little hatchet, and gold is very soft to cut. Over she goes."

"You never can upset that statue," declared Ned.

"Yes, I can," cried the young inventor. "I brought a long, thin, but very strong rope with

me, and I think if we all pull together we can
do it."

Tom made a noose and skillfully threw it over
the head of the statue. It settled about the neck,
and then, all taking hold, and walking away a
short distance, they gave a "long pull, a strong
pull, and a pull altogether."

At first the statue would not move, but when
they strained on the rope, the image suddenly
tilted, and, a moment later it tumbled to the stone
pavement. But the fall was not as heavy as should
have resulted from a statue of solid metal. There
was a tinkling sound.

"That's queer!" cried Tom. "It didn't make
half the fuss I expected," and he hurried up to
look at the fallen statue. "Why!" he cried in
astonishment, "it's hollow—the big golden statue
is hollow—it's a fake!"

And so it was. The big image was only a shell
of gold.

"Not so valuable as it looked," commented Ned.
"We could take that with us in the balloon, if it
wan't so big."

"Well, here goes for the head, anyhow!" exclaimed Tom, and with a few blows of his keen
little axe he severed the neck. As he held it up
for all to see—rather a grewsome sight it was,
too, in the flickering light of the gas torches—

there sounded throughout the underground city, a dull, booming noise, like distant thunder.

"What's that?" cried Ned.

"Bless my bath sponge!" exclaimed Mr. Damon, "I hope the water isn't rising in the river."

"Oh land a massy!" gasped Eradicate.

Without a word Tom dropped the golden head and made for the street that led to the tunnel. The others followed, and soon caught up to the young inventor. On and on they ran, with only the light of their electric flash torches to guide them. Suddenly Tom stopped.

"Go on!" cried Ned. "See what's happened! Go on!"

"I can't," answered Tom, and they all wondered at his voice. "There's a big block of stone across the tunnel, and I can't go another step. The stone gate has fallen. We're trapped here in the underground city of gold!"

"Bless my soul! The tunnel closed?" cried Mr. Damon.

"Look," said Tom simply and in hopeless tones, as he flashed his light. And there, completely filling the tunnel, was a great block of stone, fitting from ceiling to floor and from side wall to side wall, completely cutting off all escape.

"Trapped!" gasped Ned. "The Mexicans or Andy Foger did this."

"No, I don't think so," spoke Tom solemnly. "I think the pulling down of the statue released this stone gate. We trapped ourselves. Oh, why didn't I leave the statue alone!"

"That can't have done it!" declared Ned.

"We can soon tell," spoke Mr. Damon. "Let's go back and look. Later maybe we can raise the block," and they returned to the fallen gold statue, Tom casting back a hopeless look at the barrier that had buried them alive in the city of gold.

CHAPTER XXIII

"Is it a rescue?"

"Can you see anything, Tom? Any lever or anything by which we can raise the stone gate?"

It was Ned who spoke, and he addressed his chum, who was closely examining the pedestal of the fallen golden statue.

"Bless my soul!" exclaimed Mr. Damon, "we've got to find some way out of here soon— or——"

He did not finish the sentence, but they all knew what he meant.

"Oh good landy!" cried Eradicate. "What's gwine t' become ob us?"

"Don't you see anything, Tom?" repeated Ned.

"Not a thing. Not a sign of a lever or handle by which the stone might be raised. But wait, I'm going to get on top of the pedestal."

He managed to scramble up by stepping on and clinging to various ornamental projections, and soon gained the flat place where the big golden statue had rested. But he saw at a glance that it was as smooth as a billiard table.

194

"Nothing here!" he called down to Ned.

"Then how do you suppose the gate closed down when the statue was pulled off? asked Ned.

"It must have been because of the disturbance of the equilibrium, or due to a change of weight. Probably this pedestal rests on a platform, like the platform of a large scale. Its weight, with that of the statue, rested on certain concealed levers, and held the stone up out of sight in the roof of the tunnel. When I yanked down the statue I made the weight uneven, and the stone fell, and there doesn't seem to be any way of putting the weight back again."

"No, we never could get the statue back on the pedestal," said Ned. "But maybe there's some mechanism at the stone gate, or near it, like the black knob which turned off the water. We may be able to work that and raise the big stone slab."

"It's the only thing to try, as long as we haven't dynamite to blast it," agreed Tom. "Come on, we'll take a look."

They went back to where the rock closed the tunnel, but a long and frantic search failed to show the least projection, lever, handle or any other thing, that could be moved.

"What in the world do you suppose those ancients made such a terrible contrivance for?" Ned wanted to know.

"Well, if we could read the warning on the statue we might know," replied Mr. Damon. "That probably says that whoever disturbs the statue will close up the golden city forever."

"Maybe there's another way out—or in," suggested Tom hopefully. "We didn't look for that. It must be our next move. We must not let a single chance go by. We'll look for some way of getting out, at the far end of this underground city."

Filled with gloomy and foreboding thoughts, they walked away from the stone barrier. To search for another means of egress would take some time, and the same fear came to all of them —could they live that long?

"It was a queer thing, to make that statue hollow," mused Ned as he walked between Mr. Damon and Tom. "I wonder why it was done, when all the others are solid gold?"

"Maybe they found they couldn't melt up, and cast in a mould, enough gold to make a solid statue that size," suggested Mr. Damon. "Then, too, there may have been no means of getting it on the pedestal if they made it too heavy."

They discussed these and other matters as they hurried on to seek for some way of escape. In fact to talk seemed to make them less gloomy and sad, and they tried to keep up their spirits.

For several hours they searched eagerly for some means of getting out of the underground city. They went to the farthest limits of it, and found it to be several miles in diameter, but eventually they came to solid walls of stone which reached from roof to ceiling, and there was no way out.

They found that the underground city was exactly like an overturned bowl, or an Esquimo ice hut, hollow within, and with a tunnel leading to it—but all below the surface of the earth. The city had been hollowed out of solid rock, and there was but one way in or out, and that was closed by the seamless stone.

"There's no use hunting any longer," declared Tom, when, weary and footsore, they had completed a circuit of the outer circumference of the city, "the rock passage is our only hope."

"And that's no hope at all!" declared Ned.

"Yes, we must try to raise that stone slab, or —break it!" cried Tom desperately. "Come on."

"Wait a bit," advised Mr. Damon. "Bless my dinner plate! but I'm hungry. We brought some food along, and my advice to you is to eat and keep up our strength. We'll need it."

"By golly gracious, that's so!" declared Eradicate. "I'll git de eatin's."

Fortunately there was a goodly supply, and,

going in one of the houses they ate off a table of solid gold, and off dishes of the precious, yellow metal. Yet they would have given it all—yes, even the gold in their dirigible balloon—for a chance for freedom.

"I wonder what became of the chaps who used to live here?" mused Ned as he finished the rather frugal meal.

"Oh, they probably died—from a plague maybe, or there may have been a war, or the people may have risen in revolt and killed them off," suggested Tom grimly.

"But then there ought to be some remains—some mummies or skeletons or something."

"I guess every one left this underground city—every soul," suggested Mr. Damon, "and then they turned on the river and left it. I shouldn't be surprised but what we are the first persons to set foot here in thousands of years."

"And *we* may stay here for a thousand years," predicted Tom.

"Oh, good land a' massy; doan't say dat!" cried Eradicate "Why we'll all be dead ob starvation in dat time."

"Before then, I guess," muttered Tom. "I wonder if there's any water in this hole?"

"We'll need it—soon," remarked Ned, looking

at the scanty supply they had brought in with
them. "Let's have a hunt for it."

"Let Rad do that, while we work on the stone
gate," proposed the young inventor. "Rad, chase
off and see if you can find some water."

While the colored man was gone, Tom, Ned
and Mr. Damon went back to the stone gate. To
attack it without tools, or some powerful blasting
powder seemed useless, but their case was des-
perate and they knew they must do something.

"We'll try chipping away the stone at the base,"
suggested Tom. "It isn't a very hard rock, in fact
it's a sort of soft marble, or white sand stone,
and we may be able to cut out a way under the
slab door with our knifes."

Fortunately they had knives with big, strong
blades, and as Tom had said, the stone was comparatively soft. But, after several hours' work
they only had a small depression under the stone
door.

"At this rate it will take a month," sighed Ned.

"Say!" cried Tom, "we're foolish. "We should
try to cut through the stone slab itself. It can't
be so very thick. And another thing, I'm going
to play the flames from the gas torches on the
stone. The fire will make it brittle and it will
chip off easier."

This was so, but even with that advantage they

had only made a slight impression on the solid stone door after more than four hours of work, and Eradicate came back, with a hopeless look on his face, to report that he had been unable to find water.

"Then we've got to save every drop of what we've got declared Tom. "Short rations for everybody."

"And our lights, too," added Mr. Damon. "We must save them."

"All out but one!" cried Tom quickly. "If we're careful we can make them gas torches last a week, and the electric flashes are good for several days yet."

Then they laid out a plan of procedure, and divided the food into as small rations as would support life. It was grim work, but it had to be done. They found, with care, that they might live for four days on the food and water and then——

Well—no one liked to think about it.

"We must take turns chipping away at the stone door," decided Tom. "Some of us will work and some will sleep—two and two, I guess."

This plan was also carried out, and Tom and Eradicate took the first trick of hacking away at the door.

How they managed to live in the days that followed they could never tell clearly afterward. It was like some horrible nightmare, composed of hours of hacking away at the stone, and then of eating sparingly, drinking more sparingly, and resting, to get up, and do it all over again.

Their water was the first to give out, for it made them thirsty to cut at the stone, and parched mouths and swollen tongues demanded moisture. They did manage to find a place where a few drops of water trickled through the rocky roof, and without this they would have died before five days had passed.

They even searched, at times for another way out of the city of gold, for Tom had insisted there must be a way, as the air in the underground cave remained so fresh. But there must have been a secret way of ventilating the place, as no opening was found, and they went back to hacking at the stone.

Just how many days they spent in their horrible golden prison they never really knew. Tom said it was over a week, Ned insisted it was a month, Mr. Damon two months, and Eradicate pitifully said "it seem mos' laik a yeah, suah!"

It must have been about eight days, and at the end of that time there was not a scrap of food left, and only a little water. They were barely alive, and could hardly wield the knives against the stone slab. They had dug a hole about a foot deep in it, but it would have to be made much larger before any one could crawl through, even when it penetrated to the other side. And how soon this would be they did not know.

It was about the end of the eighth day, and Tom and Ned were hacking away at the rocky slab, for Mr. Damon and Eradicate were too weary.

Tom paused for a moment to look helplessly at his chum. As he did so he heard, amid the silence, a noise on the other side of the stone door.

"What—what's that?" Tom gasped faintly.

"It sounds—sounds like some one—coming," whispered Ned. "Oh, if it is only a rescue party!"

"A rescue party?" whispered Tom. "Where would a rescue party——"

He stopped suddenly. Unmistakably there were voices on the other side of the barrier—human voices.

"It *is* a rescue party!" cried Ned.

"I—I hope so," spoke Tom slowly.

"Mr. Damon—Eradicate!" yelled Ned with the sudden strength of hope, "they're coming to save us! Hurry over here!"

And then, as he and Tom stood, they saw, with staring eyes, the great stone slab slowly beginning to rise!

CHAPTER XXIV

THE FIGHT

THE talk sounded more plainly now—a confused murmur of voices—many of them—the sound coming under the slowly raising stone doorway.

"Who can it be—there's a lot of them," murmured Ned.

Tom did not answer. Instead he silently sped back to where they had slept and got his automatic revolver.

"Better get yours," he said to his companions. "It may be a rescue party, though I don't see how any one could know we were in here, or it may be——"

He did not finish. They all knew what he meant, and a moment later four strained and anxious figures stood on the inner side of the stone door, revolvers in hand, awaiting what might be revealed to them. Would it be friend or foe?

At Tom's feet lay the golden head—the hollow

head of the statue. The scene was illumined by a flickering gas torch—the last one, as the others had burned out.

Slowly the stone went up, very slowly, for it was exceedingly heavy and the mechanism that worked it was primitive. Up and up it went until now a man could have crawled under. Ned made a motion as if he was going to do so, but Tom held him back.

Slowly and slowly it went up. On the other side was a very babble of voices now—voices speaking a strange tongue. Tom and his companions were silent.

Then, above the other voices, there sounded the tones of some one speaking English. Hearing it Tom started, and still more as he noted the tones, for he heard this said:

We'll be inside in a minute, dad, and I guess we'll show Tom Swift that he and his crowd can't fool us. We've got to the city of gold first!"

"Andy Foger!" hoarsely whispered Tom to Ned.

The next moment the stone gate went up with a rush, and there, in the light of the gas torch, and in the glare of many burning ones of wood, held by a throng of people on the other side, stood Andy Foger, his father, Delazes, and a horde of men who looked as wild as savages.

For a moment both parties stood staring at one another, too startled to utter a sound. Then as Tom noticed that some of the natives, who somewhat resembled the ancient Aztecs, had imitation human heads stuck on the ends of poles or spears, he uttered two words;

"Head-hunters!"

Like a flash there came to him the warning of the African missionary: "Beware of the head-hunters!" Now they were here—being led on by the Mexican and the Fogers—the enemies of our friends.

For another moment there was a silence, and then Andy Foger cried out:

"They're here! Tom Swift and his party! They got here first and they may have all the gold!"

"If they have they will share it with us!" cried Delazes fiercely.

"Quick!" Tom called hoarsely to Ned, Mr. Damon and Eradicate. "We've got to fight. It's the only way to save our lives. We must fight, and when we can, escape, get to the airship and sail away. It's a fight to the finish now."

He raised his automatic revolver, and, as he did so one of the savages saw the golden head of the statue lying at Tom's feet. The man uttered a wild cry and called out something in his unknown tongue. Then he raised his spear and hurled it straight at our hero.

Had not Mr. Damon pulled Tom to one side, there might have been a different ending to this story. As it was the weapon hissed through the air over the head of the young inventor. The next minute his revolver spat lead and fire, but whether he hit any one or not he could not see, as the place was so filled with smoke, from the powder and from the torches. But some one yelled in pain.

"Crouch down and fire!" ordered Tom. "Low down and they'll throw over our heads." It was done on the instant, and the four revolvers rang out together.

There were howls of pain and terror and above them could be heard the gutteral tones of Delazes, while Andy Foger yelled:

"Look out dad! Here, help me to get behind something or I may be hit. Mr. Delazes, can't you tell those savages to throw spears at Tom Swift and his gang?"

"They are doing it, Senor Foger," replied the Mexican. "Oh, why did I not think to bring my gun! We haven't one among us." Then he called some command to the head-hunters who had apparently been enlisted on the side of himself and the two Fogers.

The automatic revolvers were soon emptied, and the place was now so full of smoke that neither party could see the other. The torches burned with a red glare.

"Reload!" ordered Tom, "and we'll make a rush for it! We can't keep this up long!"

It took but an instant to slip in another lot of cartridges and then, on Tom's advice, they slipped the catches to make the automatic weapons simple ones, to be fired at will.

They sent several more shots through the doorway but no cries of pain followed, and it was evident that their enemies had stepped back out of the line of fire.

"Now's our chance!" cried Tom. "The way is clear. Come on!"

He and the others dashed forward, Tom carrying the golden head, though it was hard work. It was not very heavy but it was awkward.

As they rushed through the now open gateway they crouched low to avoid the spears, but, as it was one grazed Tom's shoulder, and Eradicate was pierced in the fleshy part of his arm.

"Forward! Forward!" cried Tom. "Come on!"

And on they went, through the smoke and darkness, Ned flashing his electric torch which gave only a feeble glow as the battery was almost exhausted. On and on! Now they were through the stone gateway, now out in the long tunnel.

Behind them they could hear feet running, and several spears clattered to the stone floor. Lights flickered behind them.

"If only the river bed is dry!" gasped Tom. "We may yet escape. But if they've filled the channel——"

He did not dare think of what that would mean as he ran on, turning occasionally to fire, for he and the others had again reloaded their revolvers.

CHAPTER XXV

THE ESCAPE—CONCLUSION

THE noise behind our friends increased. There were shouts of rage, yells of anger at the escape of the prey. High above the other voices were the shrill war-cries of the head-hunters—the savages with their grewsome desires.

"Can—can we make it, Tom?" panted Ned.

They were almost at the river channel now, and in another instant they had reached it.

By the feeble rays of Ned's electric torch they saw with relief that it was empty, though they would have given much to see just a trickle of water in it, for they were almost dead from thirst.

Together they climbed up the other side, and as yet their pursuers had not reached the brink. For one moment Tom had a thought of working the black knob, and flooding the channel, but he could not doom even the head-hunters, much less the Fogers and Delazes, to such a death as that would mean.

On ran Tom and his companions, but now they

could glance back and see the foremost of the other crowd dipping down into the dry channel.

"The steps! The steps!" suddenly cried Ned, when they had run a long distance, as a faint gleam of daylight beyond showed the opening beneath the stone altar. "We're safe now."

"Hardly, but a few minutes will tell," said Tom. "The balloon is in shape for a quick rise, and then we'll leave this horrible place behind."

"And all the gold, too," murmured Ned regretfully.

"We've got some," said Mr. Damon, "and I wouldn't take a chance with those head-hunters for all the gold in the underground city."

"Same here!" panted Tom. Then they were at the steps and ran up them.

Out into the big auditorium they emerged, weak and faint, and toward the hidden dirigible balloon they rushed.

"Quick!" cried Tom, as he climbed into the car, followed by Mr. Damon and Eradicate. "Shove it right under the broken dome, Ned, and I'll turn on the gas machine. It's partly inflated."

A moment later the balloon was right below the big opening. The blue sky showed through it—a welcome sight to our friends. The hiss of the gas was heard, and the bag distended still more.

"Hop in!" cried Tom. "She'll go up I guess."

"There they come!" shouted Ned, as he spoke the foremost of the head-hunters emerged from the hole beneath the stone altar. He was followed by Delazes.

"Stop them! Get them! Spear them!" cried the contractor. They evidently thought our friends had all the gold from the underground city.

Fortunately the temple was so large that the balloon was a good distance from the hole leading to the tunnel, and before the foremost of the head-hunters could reach it the dirigible began to rise.

"If they throw their spears, and puncture the bag in many places we're done for," murmured Tom. But evidently the savages did not think of this, though Delazes screamed it at them.

Up went the balloon, and not a moment too soon, for one of the head-hunters actually grabbed the edge of the car, and only let go when he found himself being lifted off the temple floor.

Up and up it went and, as it was about to emerge from the broken dome, Tom looked down and saw a curious sight.

Mr. Foger and Andy, who brought up in the

rear of the pursuing and attacking party, had just emerged from the hole by the great stone altar when there suddenly spouted from the same opening a solid column of water. A cry of wonder came from all as they saw the strange sight. A veritable geyser was now spurting in the very middle of the temple floor, and the head-hunters, the Mexicans and the Fogers ran screaming to get out of the way.

"Look!" cried Ned. "What happened?"

"The underground river must be running the wrong way!" answered Tom, as he prepared to set in motion the motor. "Either they accidently turned some hidden lever, or when they raised the stone door they did it. The tunnel is flooded and——"

"Bless my match box! So is the underground city!" cried Mr. Damon. "I guess we've seen the last of it and its gold. We were lucky to escape with our lives, and those fellows might have been drowned like rats in a trap, if they hadn't followed us. The underground city will never be discovered again."

"And now for home!" cried Tom, when they had eaten and drunk sparingly until they should get back their strength, and had seen to their slight wounds.

"And our trip wasn't altogether a failure,"

said Mr. Damon. "We'd have had more gold if
the stone door hadn't trapped us. But I guess
we have enough as it is. I wonder how the
Fogers ever found us?"

"They must have followed our trail, though
how we'll never know and they came up to where
Delazes and his men were, joined forces with
them, and hunted about until they found the temple," remarked Tom. "Then they saw the opening, went down, and found the stone door."

"But how did they get it open? and what were
they doing with the head-hunters, and why didn't
the head-hunters attack them?" Ned wanted to
know.

"Well, I guess perhaps Delazes knew how to
handle those head-hunters," replied Tom. "They
may be a sort of lost tribe of Mexicans, and perhaps their ancestors centuries ago owned the city
of gold. At any rate I think some of them knew
the secret of raising the door." And later Tom
learned in a roundabout way from the Fogers
that this was so. The father and son had after
much hardship joined forces with Delazes and he,
by a promise of the heads of the party of our
friends, and much tobacco, had gained the head-
hunters as allies.

On and on sailed the balloon and our friends
regained their strength after partaking of the

nourishing food. They looked at their store of gold and found it larger than they had thought. Soon they left far behind them the great plain of the ruined temple, which, had they but known it was a lake now, for the underground river, perhaps by some break in the underground mechanism that controlled it, or a break in the channel, overflowed and covered temple, plain and underground city with water many fathoms deep.

"Are we going all the way home in the balloon?" asked Ned on the second day of their voyage in the air, when they had stopped to make slight repairs.

"No, indeed," replied Tom. "As soon as we get to some city where we can pack it up, and ship our gold without fear of being robbed, I'm coming to earth, and go home in a steamer."

This plan was carried out; and a week later, with the gold safely insured by an express company, and the balloon packed for transportation, our friends went to a railroad station, and took a train for Tampico, there to get a steamer for New York.

"Bless my top knot!" exclaimed Mr. Damon a few days after this, as they were on the vessel. "I think for queer adventures this one of ours in the city of gold, Tom, puts it all over the others we had."

"Oh, I don't know," answered the young inventor, "we certainly had some strenuous times in the past, and I hope we'll have some more in the future."

"The same here," agreed Ned.

And whether they did or not I will leave my readers to judge if they peruse the next book in this series, which will be called, "Tom Swift and His Air Glider; Or, Seeking the Platinum Treasure."

They arrived safely in Shopton in due course of time, and found Mr. Swift well. They did not become millionaires, for they found, to their regret that their gold was rather freely alloyed with baser metals, so they did not have more than half the amount in pure solid gold. But there was a small fortune in it for all of them.

In recognition of Mr. Illingway, the African missionary having put Tom on the track of the gold, a large sum was sent to him, to help him carry on his work of humanity.

Tom had many offers for the big golden head, but he would not sell it, though he loaned it to a New York museum, where it attracted much attention. There were many articles written about the underground city of gold from the facts the young inventor furnished.

Eventually the Fogers got home, but they did

not say much about their experiences, and Tom and his friends did not think it worth while to prosecute them for the attack. As for Delazes, Tom never saw nor heard from him again, not in all his reading could he find any account of the head-hunters, who must have been a small, little known tribe.

"And you really kept your promise, and brought me a golden image?" asked Mary Nestor of Tom, when he called on her soon after reaching home.

"Indeed I did, the two that I promised and a particularly fine one that I picked up almost at the last minute," and Tom gave her the valuable relics.

"And now tell me about it," she begged, when she had admired them, and then sat down beside Tom; and there we will leave our hero for the present, as he is in very good company, and I know he wouldn't like to be disturbed.

THE END

THE TOM SWIFT SERIES

By VICTOR APPLETON

12mo. CLOTH. UNIFORM STYLE OF BINDING. COLORED WRAPPERS,

These spirited tales convey in a realistic way the wonderful advances in land and sea locomotion. Stories like these are impressed upon the memory and their reading is productive only of good.

TOM SWIFT AND HIS MOTOR CYCLE
Or Fun and Adventure on the Road

TOM SWIFT AND HIS MOTOR BOAT
Or The Rivals of Lake Carlopa

TOM SWIFT AND HIS AIRSHIP
Or The Stirring Cruise of the Red Cloud

TOM SWIFT AND HIS SUBMARINE BOAT
Or Under the Ocean for Sunken Treasure

TOM SWIFT AND HIS ELECTRIC RUNABOUT
Or The Speediest Car on the Road

TOM SWIFT AND HIS WIRELESS MESSAGE
Or The Castaways of Earthquake Island

TOM SWIFT AMONG THE DIAMOND MAKERS
Or The Secret of Phantom Mountain

TOM SWIFT IN THE CAVES OF ICE
Or The Wreck of the Airship

TOM SWIFT AND HIS SKY RACER
Or The Quickest Flight on Record

TOM SWIFT AND HIS ELECTRIC RIFLE
Or Daring Adventures in Elephant Land

TOM SWIFT IN THE CITY OF GOLD
Or Marvellous Adventures Underground

TOM SWIFT AND HIS AIR GLIDER
Or Seeking the Platinum Treasure

TOM SWIFT IN CAPTIVITY
Or A Daring Escape by Airship

TOM SWIFT AND HIS WIZARD CAMERA
Or The Perils of Moving Picture Taking

TOM SWIFT AND HIS GREAT SEARCHLIGHT
Or On the Border for Uncle Sam

TOM SWIFT AND HIS GIANT CANNON
Or The Longest Shots on Record

TOM SWIFT AND HIS PHOTO TELEPHONE
Or The Picture that Saved a Fortune

TOM SWIFT AND HIS AERIAL WARSHIP
Or The Naval Terror of the Seas

TOM SWIFT AND HIS BIG TUNNEL
Or The Hidden City of the Andes

GROSSET & DUNLAP, PUBLISHERS NEW YORK

THE OUTDOOR CHUMS SERIES

By CAPTAIN QUINCY ALLEN

The outdoor chums are four wide-awake lads, sons of wealthy men of a small city located on a lake. The boys love outdoor life, and are greatly interested in hunting, fishing, and picture taking. They have motor cycles, motor boats, canoes, etc., and during their vacations go everywhere and have all sorts of thrilling adventures. The stories give full directions for camping out, how to fish, how to hunt wild animals and prepare the skins for stuffing, how to manage a canoe, how to swim, etc. Full of the spirit of outdoor life.

THE OUTDOOR CHUMS
Or The First Tour of the Rod, Gun and Camera Club.

THE OUTDOOR CHUMS ON THE LAKE
Or Lively Adventures on Wildcat Island.

THE OUTDOOR CHUMS IN THE FOREST
Or Laying the Ghost of Oak Ridge.

THE OUTDOOR CHUMS ON THE GULF
Or Rescuing the Lost Balloonists.

THE OUTDOOR CHUMS AFTER BIG GAME
Or Perilous Adventures in the Wilderness.

THE OUTDOOR CHUMS ON A HOUSEBOAT
Or The Rivals of the Mississippi.

THE OUTDOOR CHUMS IN THE BIG WOODS
Or The Rival Hunters at Lumber Run.

THE OUTDOOR CHUMS AT CABIN POINT
Or The Golden Cup Mystery.

12mo. Averaging 240 pages. Illustrated. Handsomely bound in Cloth.

GROSSET & DUNLAP, PUBLISHERS, NEW YORK